THE EVERYTHING®

Christmas
STORIES

MINI BOOK

Adams Media Corporation

Avon, Massachusetts

An Everything® Series Book.
"Everything" is a registered trademark of Adams Media Corporation.

Published by Adams Media Corporation
57 Littlefield Street, Avon, MA 02322
www.adamsmedia.com

ISBN: 1-58062-545-2

Printed in Canada.

J I H G F E D C B A

Library of Congress Cataloging-in-Publication Data
available from the publisher.

This publication is designed to provide accurate and authoritative information with
regard to the subject matter covered. It is sold with the understanding that the
publisher is not engaged in rendering legal, accounting, or other professional
advice. If legal advice or other expert assistance is required, the services of a
competent professional person should be sought.
    — From a *Declaration of Principles* jointly adopted by a Committee of the
American Bar Association and a Committee of Publishers and Associations

Cover illustrations by Barry Littmann.
Interior illustrations by Barry Littmann and Kathie Kelleher.

This book is available at quantity discounts for bulk purchases.
For information, call 1-800-872-5627.

Visit the entire Everything® series at everything.com

Table of Contents

4

The Little Women's Christmas

Louisa May Alcott

Published in 1868, Little Women was an instant success, particularly with female readers of the time. "The Little Women's Christmas" is an excerpt of the book's first two chapters, "Playing Pilgrims" and "A Merry Christmas." The little women themselves stand as a reminder to all who have endured hard times that even a penniless Christmas can be cause for celebration . . . if it is filled with selfless generosity, love, and faith.

"CHRISTMAS WON'T BE Christmas without any presents," grumbled Jo, lying on the rug.

"It's so dreadful to be poor!" sighed Meg, looking down at her old dress.

"I don't think it's fair for some girls to have lots of pretty things, and other girls nothing at all," added little Amy, with an injured sniff.

"We've got father, and mother, and each other, anyhow," said Beth, contentedly, from her corner.

The four young faces on which the firelight shone brightened at the cheerful words, but darkened again as Jo said sadly, "We haven't got father, and shall not have him for a long time." She didn't say "perhaps never," but each silently added it, thinking of father far away, where the fighting was.

Nobody spoke for a minute; then Meg said in an altered tone, "You know the reason mother

proposed not having any presents this Christmas was because it's going to be a hard winter for everyone; and she thinks we ought not to spend money for pleasure, when our men are suffering so in the army. We can't do much, but we can make our little sacrifices, and ought to do it gladly. But I am afraid I don't," and Meg shook her head, as she thought regretfully of all the pretty things she wanted.

"But I don't think the little we should spend would do any good. We've each got a dollar, and the army wouldn't be much helped by our giving that. I agree not to expect anything from mother or you, but I do want to buy *Undine and Sintram* for myself: I've wanted it *so* long," said Jo, who was a bookworm.

"I planned to spend mine on new music," said Beth, with a little sigh, which no one heard but the hearth brush and kettleholder.

"I shall get a nice box of Faber's drawing pencils; I really need them," said Amy decidedly.

"Mother didn't say anything about our money, and she won't wish us to give up everything. Let's each buy what we want, and have a little fun; I'm sure we grub hard enough to earn it," cried Jo, examining the heels of her boots in a gentlemanly manner.

"I know *I* do—teaching those dreadful children nearly all day, when I'm longing to enjoy myself at home," began Meg, in the complaining tone again.

"You don't have half such a hard time as I do," said Jo. "How would you like to be shut up for hours with a nervous, fussy old lady, who keeps you trotting, is never satisfied, and worries you till you're ready to fly out of the window or box her ears?"

"It's naughty to fret, but I do think washing dishes and keeping

things tidy is the worst work in the world. It makes me cross; and my hands get so stiff, I can't practice good a bit." Beth looked at her rough hands with a sign that anyone could hear that time.

"I don't believe any of you suffer as I do," cried Amy; "for you don't have to go to school with impertinent girls, who plague you if you don't know your lessons, and laugh at your dresses, and label your father if he isn't rich, and insult you when your nose isn't nice."

"If you mean *libel* I'd say so, and not talk about *labels*, as if Pa was a pickle-bottle," advised Jo, laughing.

"I know what I mean, and you needn't be 'statirical' about it. It's proper to use good words, and improve your *vocabilary*," returned Amy, with dignity.

"Don't peck at one another, children," said Meg.

It was a comfortable old room, though the carpet was faded and the furniture very plain, for a

good picture or two hung on the walls, books filled the recesses, chrysanthemums and Christmas roses bloomed in the windows, and a pleasant atmosphere of home peace pervaded it.

Margaret, the eldest of four, was 16, and very pretty. Fifteen-year-old Jo was tall, thin, and brown, and reminded one of a colt; for she never seemed to know what to do with her long limbs, which were very much in her way. Elizabeth—or Beth, as everyone called her—was a rosy, smooth-haired, bright-eyed girl of 13. Amy, though the youngest, was a most important person, in her own opinion at least.

The clock struck six; and, having swept up the hearth, Beth put a pair of slippers down to warm.

 Somehow the sight of the old shoes had a good effect upon the girls, for Mother was coming, and everyone bright-ened to welcome her.

"They are quite worn out; Marmee must have a new pair."

"I thought I'd get her some with my dollar," said Beth.

"No, I shall!" cried Amy.

"I'm the oldest," began Meg, but Jo cut in with a decided—"I'm the man of the family, now Papa is away, and *I* shall provide the slippers, for he told me to take special care of Mother while he was gone."

"I'll tell you what we'll do," said Beth; "let's each get her something for Christmas, and not get anything for ourselves."

"That's like you, dear! What will we get?" exclaimed Jo.

Everyone thought soberly for a minute; then Meg announced, as if the idea was suggested by the sight of her own pretty hands, "I shall give her a nice pair of gloves."

"Army shoes, best to be had," cried Jo.

"Some handkerchiefs, all hemmed," said Beth.

"I'll get a little bottle of cologne; she likes it, and it won't cost much, so I'll have some left to buy something for me," added Amy.

"How will we give the things?" asked Meg.

"Put 'em on the table, and bring her in and see her open the bundles," answered Jo.

"Well, dearies, how have you got on today?" said a cheery voice at the door. "There was so much to do, getting the boxes ready to go tomorrow, that I didn't come home to dinner. Has anyone called, Beth? How is your cold, Meg? Jo, you look tired to death. Come and kiss me, baby."

While making these maternal inquiries, Mrs. March got her wet things off, her hot slippers on, and sitting down in the easy chair, drew Amy to her lap, preparing to enjoy the happiest hour of her busy day. The girls flew about, trying to make things comfortable, each in her own way. Meg arranged the tea table; Jo brought wood and set

chairs, dropping, overturning, and clattering everything she touched; Beth trotted to and fro
between parlor and kitchen, quiet and busy; while
Amy gave directions to everyone, as she sat with
her hands folded.

As they gathered about the table, Mrs. March
said, with a particularly happy face, "I've got a
treat for you after supper."

A quick, bright smile went round like a
streak of sunshine. Beth clapped her hands,
regardless of the hot biscuit she held and Jo
tossed up her napkin, crying, "A letter! A letter!
Three cheers for Father!"

"Yes, a nice long letter. He is well, and
thinks he shall get through the cold
season better than we feared. He
sends all sorts of loving
wishes for Christmas, and
an especial message to
our girls," said Mrs.

March, patting her pocket as if she had got a treasure there.

"Hurry up, and get done. Don't stop to quirk your little finger, and prink over your plate, Amy," cried Jo, choking in her tea, and dropping her bread, butter side down, on the carpet, in her haste to get at the treat.

Beth ate no more, but crept away, to sit in her shadowy corner and brood over the delight to come, till the others were ready.

"I think it was so splendid in Father to go as a chaplain when he was too old to be drafted, and not strong enough for a soldier," said Meg, warmly.

"When will he come home, Marmee?" asked Beth, with a little quiver in her voice.

"Not for many months, dear, unless he is sick. He will stay and do his work faithfully as long as he can, and we won't ask for him

back a minute sooner than he can be spared. Now come and hear the letter."

They all drew to the fire, Mother in the big chair with Beth at her feet, Meg and Amy perched on either arm of the chair, and Jo leaning on the back, where no one would see any sign of emotion if the letter should happen to be touching.

Very few letters were written in those hard times that were not touching, especially those which fathers sent home. In this one little was said of the hardships endured, the dangers faced, or the homesickness conquered; it was a cheerful, hopeful letter, full of lively descriptions of camp life, marches, and military news; and only at the end did the writer's heart overflow with fatherly love and longing for the little girls at home.

"Give them all my dear love and a kiss. Tell them I think of them by day, pray for them by night, and find my best comfort in their affection at all times. A year seems very long to wait before

I see them, but remind them that while we wait
we may all work, so that these hard days need not
be wasted. I know they will remember all I said to
them, that they will be loving children to you, will
do their duty faithfully, fight their bosom enemies
bravely, and conquer themselves so beautifully, that
when I come back to them I may be fonder and
prouder than ever of my little women."

Everybody sniffed when they came to that
part; Jo wasn't ashamed of the great tear that
dropped off the end of her nose, and Amy never
minded the rumpling of her curls as she hid her
face on her mother's shoulder and sobbed out, "I
am a selfish pig! but I'll truly try to be better, so
he mayn't be disappointed in me by and by."

"We all will!" cried Meg. "I think too much of
my looks, and hate to work, but won't any more,
if I can help it."

"I'll try and be what he loves to call me, 'a
little woman,' and not be rough and wild; but do

my duty here instead of wanting to be somewhere else," said Jo, thinking that keeping her temper at home was a much harder task than facing a rebel or two down South.

Beth said nothing, but wiped away her tears with the blue army-sock, and began to knit with all her might, losing no time in doing the duty that lay nearest her, while she resolved in her quiet little soul to be all that Father hoped to find her when the year brought round the happy coming home.

Jo was the first to wake in the gray dawn of Christmas morning. No stockings hung at the fire-place, and for a moment she felt as much disappointed as she did long ago, when her little sock fell down because it was so crammed with goodies. Then she remembered her mother's promise, and

slipping her hand under her pillow, drew out a little crimson-covered book. She knew it very well, for it was that beautiful old story of the best life ever lived, and Jo felt that it was a true guidebook for any pilgrim going the long journey. She woke Meg with a "Merry Christmas," and bade her see what was under her pillow. A green-covered book appeared, with the same picture inside, and a few words written by their mother, which made their one present very precious in their eyes. Presently Beth and Amy woke, to rummage and find their little books also—one dove-colored, the other blue—and all sat looking at and talking about them, while the East grew rosy with the coming day.

"Girls," said Meg, seriously, looking from the tumbled head beside her to the two little night-capped ones in the room beyond, "mother wants us to read and love and mind these books, and we must begin at once. We used to be faithful

about it; but since Father went away, and all this war trouble unsettled us, we have neglected many things. You can do as you please; but I shall keep my book on the table here, and read a little every morning as soon as I wake, for I know it will do me good, and help me through the day."

Then she opened her new book and began to read. Jo put her arm around her, and leaning cheek to cheek, read also, with the quiet expression so seldom seen on her restless face.

"How good Meg is! Come, Amy, let's do as they do. I'll help you with the hard words, and they'll explain things if we don't understand," whispered Beth, very impressed by the pretty books and her sister's example.

"I'm glad mine is blue," said Amy; and then the rooms were very still while the pages were softly turned, and the winter sunshine crept in to touch the bright heads and serious faces with a Christmas greeting.

"Where is Mother?" asked Meg, as she and Jo ran down to thank her for their gifts, half an hour later.

"Goodness only knows. Some poor creeter come a-beggin', and your ma went straight off to see what was needed. There never *was* such a woman for givin' away vittles and drink, clothes, and firin'," replied Hannah, who had lived with the family since Meg was born, and was considered by them all more as a friend than a servant.

"She will be back soon, I guess; so do your cakes, and have everything ready," said Meg, looking over the presents which were collected in a basket and kept under the sofa, ready to be produced at the proper time, "Why, where is Amy's bottle of cologne?" she added, as the little flask did not appear.

"She took it out a minute ago, and went off with it to put a ribbon on it, or some such

notion," replied Jo, dancing about the room to take the first stiffness off the new army-slippers.

"How nice my handkerchiefs look, don't they? Hannah washed and ironed them for me, and I marked them all myself," said Beth, looking proudly at the somewhat uneven letters which had cost her such labor.

"Bless the child, she's gone and put 'Mother' on them instead of 'M. March'; how funny!" cried Jo, taking up one.

"Isn't it right? I though it was better to do it so because Meg's initials are 'M. M.' and I don't want anyone to use these but Marmee," said Beth, looking troubled.

"It's all right, dear, and a very pretty idea; quite sensible, too, for no one can ever mistake them now. It will please her very much, I know," said Meg, with a frown for Jo, and a smile for Beth.

"There's Mother; hide the basket, quick!"
cried Jo, as a door slammed, and steps sounded
in the hall.

Amy came in hastily, and looked rather
abashed when she saw her sisters all waiting
for her.

"Where have you been, and what are you
hiding behind you? asked Meg, surprised to see,
by her hood and cloak, that lazy Amy had been
out so early.

"Don't laugh at me, Jo. I didn't mean anyone
should know till the time came. I only meant to
change the little bottle for a big one, and I gave
all my money to get it, and I'm truly trying not to
be selfish any more."

As she spoke, Amy showed the handsome
flask which replaced the cheap one; and looked
so earnest and humble in her little effort to forget
herself, that Meg hugged her on the spot, and Jo
pronounced her "a trump," while Beth ran to the

window, and picked her finest rose to ornament
the stately bottle.

"You see, I felt ashamed of my present, after
reading and talking about being good this
morning, so I ran round the corner and changed
it the minute I was up; and I'm glad, for mine is
the handsomest now."

Another bang of the street-door sent the
basket under the sofa, and the girls to the table
eager for breakfast.

"Merry Christmas, Marmee! Lot of them!
Thank you for our books; we read some, and
mean to every day," they cried in chorus.

"Merry Christmas, little daughters! I'm glad
you began at once, and hope you will keep on.
But I want to say one word
before we sit down. Not far
away from her lies a poor
woman with a little new-born
baby. Six children are huddled

into one bed to keep from freezing, for they have no fire. There is nothing to eat over there; and the oldest boy came to tell me they were suffering hunger and cold. My girls, will you give them your breakfast as a Christmas present?"

They were all unusually hungry, having waited nearly an hour, and for a minute no one spoke; only a minute, for Jo exclaimed impetuously, "I'm so glad you came before we began!"

"May I go and help carry the things to the poor little children?" asked Beth, eagerly.

"*I* shall take the cream and the muffins," added Amy, heroically giving up the articles she most liked.

Meg was already covering the buckwheats, and piling the bread into one big plate.

"I thought you'd do it," said Mrs. March, smiling as if satisfied. "You shall all go and help me, and when we come back we will have bread and milk for breakfast, and make it up at dinner-time."

They were soon ready, and the procession set out. Fortunately it was early, and they went through back streets, so few people saw them, and no one laughed at the funny party.

A poor, bare, miserable room it was, with broken windows, no fire, ragged bedclothes, a sick mother, wailing baby, and a group of pale, hungry children cuddled under one old quilt, trying to keep warm. How the big eyes stared, and the blue lips smiled, as the girls went in!

"*Ach, mein Gott!* It is good angels come to us!" cried the poor woman, crying for joy.

"Funny angels in hoods and mittens," said Jo, and set them laughing.

In a few minutes it really did seem as if kind spirits had been at work there. Hannah, who had carried wood, made a fire, and stopped up the broken panes with old hats, and her own shawl. Mrs. March gave the mother tea and gruel, and comforted her with promises of help, while she

dressed the little baby as tenderly as if it had been her own. The girls, meantime, spread the table, set the children round the fire, and fed them like so many hungry birds; laughing, talking, and trying to understand the funny broken English.

"Das ist gut! Die angel-kinder!" cried the poor things, as they ate, and warmed their purple hands at the comfortable blaze. The girls had never been called angel children before, and thought it very agreeable. That was a very happy breakfast, though they didn't get any of it; and when they went away, leaving comfort behind, I think there were not in all the city four merrier people than the hungry little girls who gave away their breakfasts, and contented themselves with bread and milk on Christmas morning.

"That's loving our neighbor better than ourselves, and I like it," said Meg, as they set out their presents, while their mother was upstairs collecting clothes for the poor Hummels.

Not a very splendid show, but there was a great deal of love done up in the few little bundles; and the tall vase of red roses, white chrysanthemums, and trailing vines, which stood in the middle, gave quite an elegant air to the table.

"She's coming! Strike up, Beth. Open the door, Amy. Three cheers for Marmee!" cried Jo, prancing about, while Meg went to conduct Mother to the seat of honor.

Beth played her gayest march, Amy threw open the door, and Meg enacted escort with great dignity. Mrs. March was both surprised and touched; and smiled with her eyes full as she examined her presents, and read the little notes which accompanied them.
The slippers went on at
once, a new handkerchief
was slipped into her
pocket, well scented with
Amy's cologne, the rose

was fastened in her bosom, and the nice gloves were pronounced "a perfect fit."

There was a good deal of laughing, and kissing, and explaining, in the simple, loving fashion which makes these home festivals so pleasant at the time and so sweet to remember long afterward.

Beth nestled up to her mother, and whispered softly, "I'm afraid Father isn't having such a merry Christmas as we are."

The Little Match Girl

Hans Christian Anderson

Reflecting the poverty from which Andersen himself came, "The Little Match Girl" offers us a heroine who shows how faith makes it possible to transcend the hardships of everyday life. The story has become one of the timeless classics of the holidays.

T WAS TERRIBLY COLD and nearly dark on the last evening of the old year, and the snow was falling fast. In the cold and the darkness, a poor little girl, with bare head and naked feet, roamed through the streets. It is true she had on a pair of slippers when she left home, but they were not of much use. They were very large, so large, indeed, that they had belonged to her mother, and the poor little creature had lost them in running across the street to avoid two carriages that were rolling along at a terrible rate. One of the slippers she could not find, and a boy seized upon the other and ran away with it, saying that he could use it as a cradle, when he had children of his own.

So the little girl went on with her little naked feet, which were quite red and blue with the cold. In an old apron she carried a number of matches, and had a bundle of them in her

hands. No one had bought anything of her the whole day, nor had anyone given her even a penny. Shivering with cold and hunger, she crept along; poor little child, she looked the picture of misery. The snowflakes fell on her long, fair hair, which hung in curls on her shoulders, but she regarded them not.

Lights were shining from every window, and there was a savory smell of roast-goose, for it was New Year's Eve—yes, she remembered that. In a corner, between two houses, one of which projected beyond the other, she sank down and huddled herself together. She had drawn her little feet under her, but she could not keep off the cold; and she dared not go home, for she had sold no matches and could not take home even a penny of money. Her father would certainly beat her; besides, it was almost as cold

at home as here, for they had only the roof to
cover them, through which the wind howled,
although the largest holes had been stopped up
with straw and rags.

Her little hands were almost frozen with the
cold. Ah! Perhaps a burning match might be
some good, if she could draw it from the bundle
and strike it against the wall, just to warm her fingers. She drew one out—scratch!—how it sputtered
as it burnt! It gave a warm, bright light, like a little
candle, as she held her hand over it.

It really was a wonderful light. It seemed to
the little girl that she was sitting by a large iron
stove, with polished brass feet and a brass ornament. How the fire burned! And it seemed so

beautifully warm that the
child stretched out her
feet as if to warm them,
when, lo, the flame of
the match went out, the

stove vanished, and she had only the remains of
the half-burnt match in her hand.

She rubbed another match on the wall. It
burst into flame, and where its light fell upon the
wall it became as transparent as a veil,
and she could see into the room.
The table was covered with a
snowy white tablecloth, on
which stood a splendid dinner service and a
steaming roast goose, stuffed with apples and
dried plums. And what was still more wonderful,
the goose jumped down from the dish and wad-
dled across the floor, with a knife and fork in its
breast, to the little girl. Then the match went out,
and there remained nothing but the thick, damp,
cold wall before her.

She lighted another match, and then she
found herself sitting under a beautiful Christmas
tree. It was larger and more beautifully decorated
than the one which she had seen through the

glass door at the rich merchant's. Thousands of tapers were burning upon the green branches, and colored pictures, like those she had seen in the show-windows, looked down upon it all. The little one stretched out her hand towards them, and the match went out.

The Christmas lights rose higher and higher, till they looked to her like the stars in the sky. Then she saw a star fall, leaving behind it a bright streak of fire. "Someone is dying," thought the little girl, for her old grandmother, the only one who had ever loved her, and who was now dead, had told her that when a star falls, a soul was going up to God. She again rubbed a match on the wall, and the light shone round her; in the brightness stood her old grandmother, clear and shining, yet mild and loving in her appearance. "Grandmother," cried the little one, "oh, take me with you: I know

you will go away when the match burns out; you
will vanish like the warm stove, the roast goose,
and the large, glorious Christmas tree." And she
made haste to light the whole bundle of matches,
for she wished to keep her grandmother there.
And the matches glowed with a light that was
brighter than the noon-day.

Her grandmother had never appeared so large
or so beautiful. She took the little girl in her arms,
and they both flew upwards in brightness and joy
far above the earth, where there was neither cold
nor hunger nor pain, for they were with God.

In the dawn of the morning, there lay the little
one, with pale cheeks and smiling mouth, leaning
against the wall; she had been frozen to death on
the last evening of the year, and the New Year's
sun rose and shone upon a little corpse. The child
still sat, in the stiffness of death, holding the

matches in her hand, one bundle of which was burnt. "She tried to warm herself," said some. No one imagined what beautiful things she had seen, nor into what glory she had entered with her grandmother, on New Year's Day.

The Gate

Walter Ash

Based in part on an old play by K. M. Rice, Ash's "The Gate" is a Christmas tale of loss and redemption, of incalculable pain and unforeseen renewal. It traces a fateful series of events in the lives of three people—and reminds us that there are many fewer strangers in this world than we may at first be inclined to believe.

I N A BUSY RAILROAD STATION in New York City on Christmas Eve, 1911, an announcer shouted, "Boston! Boston! First track on the left!" Not all of his intended audience understood his words.

Among the uncounted travelers milling through the huge concourse that night, one could have made out a host of tired and bedraggled immigrants from the nation that loves Christmas perhaps more fervently than any other; and among these scores of German men, women, and children, one could have made out a worried-looking woman in blue who had been separated from her party and did not know where to go, who neither spoke nor understood a word of English, and who scanned the wooden benches as she led her daughter, a little girl of

about four bearing a small bundle, through the station. If one understood German, one would have known that the young mother told her little girl not to move, that she, the mother, would return in a moment. One would have heard the child agree. One would have seen the mother struggle back into the crowd, rejoin her group, and, before she could frame the question she meant to ask about the train's departure time, find herself shoved, with the rest of the party, toward the track by the gate tender. One would have heard her shout for her child, still and sharp at first, then rising, like the shriek of tearing metal, but still a component of the general din. One would have heard many shouts, many calls, some of it in one's own language, some of it not. One would have heard the gate tender bellow to someone in the party to keep the

young mother in line, that he had seen her ticket and knew where she was bound. One would have seen the mother carried along with the crowd, her terrified voice reverberating and eventually dying away, as she was borne along toward the train, and one would have heard the chuffing of the engine, and an exhausted roar, and a grey roll toward Boston.

And one would have been able to make out, had one looked back to the far end of the sta-

tion, a little blonde girl in a dark cap who, like her mother, spoke not a word of English, seated alone with her tiny bundle on her wooden bench. One would have seen her staring ahead impassively, still, waiting expectantly for her mother as the thousands of Christmas travelers walked past.

Three little schoolgirls, home for the holiday and waiting to be met by their parents, sat down next to her. The oldest marked her and said, "She's so lovely! And look, she hasn't moved a muscle this whole time."

The next oldest said, "It's as if she's posing for a picture."

The youngest said, "She's looking for something."

Then the oldest of the three girls spied their father, and they all shouted and ran away.

Still the little girl stared at the black gate.

After a time, a man and a woman passed by the bench. The man was mustachioed, in his late 40s, tall and thin. His chin bore a week's stubble. His companion was a woman of about his age, short and stocky, with a tiny pinched-up face and a sneer that seemed to speak of a lifetime of discontent.

They passed nonchalantly several times, watching the little girl and pretending not to. From the bench across the aisle, a bespectacled woman

looked up from her newspaper and watched them suspiciously.

"She's been left behind," the tall man said to his companion. "All those Germans boarded that train for Boston. She's abandoned."

"Would you lower your voice?" the stout woman hissed. "Do you want someone to hear you? Turn around; I think that busybody over on the other bench is watching us. Now, what if her folks come back for her?"

"Every last one of those Germans got on the Boston train, I tell you."

They stood for a moment, looking away from the benches. When the woman turned back, she saw only the girl; the woman with the newspaper was nowhere to be seen.

"Let's take her, then," the woman whispered to her companion. "Get her ticket and give it to me. Then pick her up. We'll find her a new home—and profit from it."

Quickly, almost before the little girl knew what was happening, a bony hand was at her coat. It tore off the red Immigration ticket that had been pinned there. The sound of the paper tearing was followed by the little girl's shout of surprise and fear, and a few desperate words from her in German.

The man lifted her up and held her toward his companion. "Mommy will give you something to eat," he said. "Don't cry." The tiny one was indeed sobbing now, pointing toward the black gate and shouting in inexplicable bursts.

"Would you mind telling me what you two are doing with that little girl?"

The voice was not hard, but intent, a voice that was not, perhaps, accustomed to being raised, but that could be brought to bear when the occasion demanded. It belonged to a well dressed woman in her 30s with almond-colored hair tied in

a bun. Under her arm was a neatly folded newspaper. On the bridge of her nose was a small pair
of spectacles.

The man withdrew the little girl, whom he
was attempting to hand to his companion, and set
her roughly on the bench. Without bothering to
look at the stout woman with the pinched little
face, he backed away from the bench.

"I'm her mother," the stout woman said
unconvincingly.

The woman in spectacles knelt down to comfort the little girl. "Then you'd best tell her father
that the policeman at the far end of the station is
walking this way," she said. "He will be asking
you a great many questions. Be sure you can

answer them without contradicting
one another."

In an instant the man was
gone, his footsteps echoing for a
time above the din of the station.

The stout woman swore an oath, then turned and ran after the thin man.

The woman tried to comfort the weeping child. "Don't worry, little one," she said, trying to soothe the girl. "Don't worry. We will find your mother." The girl was chattering and weeping in German, staring at the black gate and pointing. Her young cheeks were bright with tears.

"Don't bother with her, ma'am," a voice from behind the woman said. She turned around to find an old railroad official in a blue uniform. "Likely enough her mother abandoned her there. These immigrants have been known to do worse, poor wretches. Down on their luck, I suppose. That was a nice piece of play-acting about the policeman, there. I suppose you'll be wanting me to call one for you now. I'm afraid it's the home for wanderers this one's bound for."

She stared at him. The little girl had begun to control her sobs, which were now tiny heaves. She would not look away from the gate.

"Thank you for the offer," came the answer. "I shall summon the police myself in a moment, once I've calmed her down. Please don't trouble yourself."

They could not understand each other. The little girl's rescuer had thought of looking for someone who could speak German, but since her young friend steadfastly refused to be moved from the spot on which she sat, finding a translator would have meant leaving the girl unattended, and that seemed unthinkable. So they sat together for a time.

Every once in a while, the little girl would point to the gate and say something in German,

confidently and even with a little pride. Although
she had no way to make out the words, the word
"mutter" sounded repeatedly, and the woman in
spectacles eventually concluded that she was
being told that the little girl's mother would return
momentarily. At length a discussion (of sorts)
ensued, and by revealing several times, and with
broad gesticulations, that her own name was
Eugenia Parsley, the woman was able, after a
number of false starts, to determine that the girl's
name was Ingrid. After a few moments, during
which the youngster had managed to stop crying
altogether, Miss Parsley withdrew a pad of paper
and a pencil and began to write.

"James," (she wrote) "it has been more
than an hour, and the young lady for whom
we're waiting has not arrived. I
have, however, encountered
someone else, someone who
needs both your assistance and

mine. Please come to meet me near the north entrance of the terminal. I am seated on one of the benches there."

"Boy!" she called. A young lad of eight or nine years turned at the call and said, "Yes, ma'am?"

"Would you care to earn a dollar?"

"A whole dollar, ma'am?"

"Yes, indeed, a whole dollar. Take this note to my driver; you'll find him in the blue and white automobile near the front entrance. Return here with him and you shall have your payment."

The boy ran off. In a few moments, he returned with a befuddled driver and an open hand. She paid the lad, who vanished into the crowd quite unable to believe his luck. Eugenia Parsley turned to her driver, who stood waiting for his instructions. "Yes, ma'am?" he said, touching his cap.

She explained the situation and, having handed the pad and pencil to James, dictated the contents of an advertisement to be placed in every German-language newspaper in the country, and every other paper, German-speaking or otherwise, in New York and Boston.

The advertisement advised that a young German girl of about four years of age answering to the name of Ingrid had been found in Central Station in New York City on Christmas Eve, having apparently been separated from her mother, and that said mother was, in the author's estimation, likely bound for Boston despite her best efforts not to be so. The readers of the advertisement were instructed to contact Miss Eugenia Parsley at her permanent address (and here she supplied the particulars of her upstate New York abode). Anyone supplying any worthwhile information, the advertisement continued, would be eligible for a cash reward of a size to be determined after the

girl was reunited with her mother. Having relayed
all this to James, whose skill at such tasks was
evident as his hand sped across page after page,
Miss Parsley looked to the little girl. She was still
staring at the black gate.

"There remains only the matter of bringing
her with us, James," she said.

James pocketed the papers and the pencil and
eyed the young girl warily. "Yes, ma'am," he said.

He took a breath, walked toward her, and
attempted, rather clumsily, to pick her up. She
screamed at once, and again began to cry and
shout incomprehensible words and point at the
black gate.

"James, I'm surprised at you," Miss Parsley
said. "You act as though you've never held a little
girl before. Put her down immediately."

James put her back gently.

Miss Parsley kneeled and looked the little girl
in the eyes. "'Mutter'?" she said softly. "Shall we

find your 'mutter'?" There was a silence. And then the little girl slid off the bench, looking all the while into Miss Parsley's hazel eyes.

The little girl took a position directly in front of her benefactress, who placed her large white hands upon the child's shoul-  ders. "James will help you. Let's go with James," Miss Parsley said.

And in a moment Miss Parsley had hoisted the little girl into the waiting arms of the driver. They had hardly moved when a little cry came from Ingrid.

"She doesn't like me, ma'am," James said, helplessly.

"Nonsense, James," said Miss Parsley. "You've only to look at her to see that she wants us to bring along her bundle."

Indeed, the little girl was pointing at the tiny bundle on the bench, her lower lip held steady,

but vibrating a little now and then. Miss Parsley
picked up the bundle and handed it to James,
and together the three made their way out of the
crowded and noisy station.

It was the late afternoon of Christmas Eve,
1927. In a small New York town, a woman with
disheveled white hair, wearing a tattered dress,
made her way down a flight of stairs with a
basket on her arm, intending to have a pleasant
sit on the front porch of the building in which
she rented a room. She had not been long in
this (or, it seemed, any) town—she had held her
lodgings for perhaps six months.
She paid her way by taking in
washing, but she did not now, nor
did she customarily, get much
work. This may have been as a

result of the fact that she was not an easy person
to talk to, or to watch, and this put her at a dis-
advantage with potential cus-
tomers. Her English was bad.
She was brusque and often
impatient. She put people off.
She gave them the feeling that she
had been too long alone and too thoroughly
broken to be at ease with others. And indeed this
may well have been the case.

In the distance she heard young voices singing:

Good King Wenceslas looked out
On the feast of Stephen
Where the snow lay round about
Deep and crisp and even.
Brightly shone the moon that night,
Though the frost was cruel,
When a poor man came in sight,
Gathering winter fuel.

She sighed. She had heard the song many times, and it always stirred her heart. She had learned the words in German when she herself was a child, of course, but now she knew and recognized the words as well as the tune. As the lyrics rang across the skies from the mouths of children, the old woman (her name was Eva) stared at the ground as she sat in her rocking chair. Her lips moved silently, framing the new English words of the old song.

The children came nearer. Although on this of all days she should have felt safe among the people of the neighborhood, and among children at that, habit died hard. She was, after all, (and she knew this, intuitively) considered the oddest resident of the neighborhood: Crazy Eva, the strange old German woman who never troubled herself to speak to anyone on the street. She had

come, by now, to believe she would always be so—
if not Crazy Eva in this town, then another such
name in another one. Before the children came
into view, she hid behind the outer stair.

Presently the children were quite near the house,
laughing and shouting about which song to sing next.
One of them asked where they had arrived.

"This," she heard a young boy's voice say, "is
where Crazy Eva lives. People call her crazy; to me
she just looks sad. I saw her sitting on the porch
once, although she didn't see me; she had a string
of beads around her neck. I do believe she was
praying. They were the kind Ingrid has, you know."

At the moment the word "Ingrid" was spoken,
Eva's breath went short.

"Perhaps she'll come out for
us," a little girl said. "Perhaps
we should sing her a carol."

"You can't be serious," an
older girl exclaimed. "It's Crazy

Eva. Who knows what she'll do to us if she comes out. Let's find another house."

"I say it's Christmas for everyone, and that includes Crazy Eva," the first little girl said emphatically. "Let's sing 'God Rest Ye Merry, Gentlemen.'"

"Yes," said the little boy who had seen Eva's beads, "'God Rest Ye Merry, Gentlemen.'" The first notes rang out—and then from behind the stair an old woman's voice said, "Dat song you have been singing. Again, please. Sing dat song for me once more, please."

And Eva stepped from the shadows and stood before the children.

The older girl, the one who had wanted to move on to another house, turned white. But she did not move. None of them moved.

For an instant all was silence, then the youngest girl, the one who had insisted on staying

(she was a radiant little one with jet-black hair),
began to sing.

> *Good King Wenceslas looked out*
> *On the feast of Stephen . . .*

she began, and the other children, every one of
them, joined in and sang the carol through again
for Eva.

At the end of the song, all the children were
staring happily at Eva, who was smiling with the
broadest smile she had smiled in 16 years.

"I like dat song the most oaf any song dere
is," said Eva. "*Auf Deutsch*—in the German—we call
it *Der Gute Konig Wenceslas.*"

The littlest one clapped her
hands joyfully and said, "Oh,
she likes Ingrid's song!"

Eva knelt down and
looked at the little girl, who for

some reason did not flinch at the sight of the fearful old lady against whom she had so often been warned in recent months.

Truth be told, Eva was only 50, but the years had not been at all kind to her.

"Dis Ingrid you are speaking off," she said slowly. "Vere does she liff?"

"Why, here in town," said the youngest girl.

"And how old, how old dis Ingrid iss?"

"Forty," said one.

"Never," said another. "She's not *that* old."

"Thirty," said another.

"You are all such geese," said the oldest girl. Ingrid is only 20. She told me so herself on her birthday. Actually, it was her *make-believe* birthday, for she hasn't a real one at all, you know. And she might as well not have Christmas either, for all the moping she does around it."

There was a pause. Eva took a deep breath
and moved closer to the oldest girl. "Tell me
please—no, no, I vill not hurt you—tell me please,
how is it this Ingrid is not vit a real birthday."

"Because she forgot it, of course. Oh, she
knew it once. But she was lost when she was a
little girl, a foolish little girl who got separated
from her own mother, you see."

"Ah."

All the little ones looked at her face; Eva
stared off into the distance. A moment passed,
and then the oldest girl looked round at the
others. She made a motion for them to leave
while Eva was in her reverie, but got no
response. The girl smirked and
scowled, then turned on her heel
and began to walk away. She had
not moved more than a step or
two when she felt Eva's gentle
hand on her shoulder.

"No, no, not yet, please, not yet," Eva said in a low voice, not at all frightening, but more as a child who cannot bear to have the evening bedtime story end so soon. "Please," she continued, "please, do not go yet. Tell me. Why is it you say she is sad always venn it is Christmas?"

The older girl stared at her for a moment but could not manage to get a word out. Finally from the back a voice piped: "Tell her, Louise."

"Because," Louise said at last, staring at the gentle eyes of her inquisitor, "it is like this, you see. When Ingrid was but a little girl, she was separated from her mother in New York . . ."

"Vit, vit de trains, vit de many, many trains . . ." Eva said softly, barely above a whisper.

Louise looked at her young companions, and then back at Eva.

"In a train station, yes. Why, that's it exactly."

Eva's hand stroked Louise's cheek slowly, then patted it gently, and then fell.

"Bring her here," Eva said. "Tell her dat I knew her mother."

For the first time in a very many years, Eva threw up her hands and laughed, not so much because she recognized her daughter as she walked towards her, but because she felt the familiar rhythm of the girl's approach. It is an interesting question, whether or not two people who are bonded as one, as parent and child, would, after an interval of a decade and a half, still respond with that instinctual knowledge of the other's pres-ence that so defines their rela-tionship. Eva's reaction to the 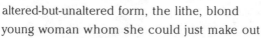 altered-but-unaltered form, the lithe, blond young woman whom she could just make out

in the distance, that reaction was unmistakable
in its joy at recognition. It was unintentional, it
was obvious before even the fea-
tures of the youngster's face were
visible. Eva's reaction, indeed,
would lead one to believe that
the bond between a mother
and a daughter is not broken by even a dense
span of time. The halting half-smile of the
young beauty herself, however, would lead one
to believe that even a mother's instinctive—if
quickly stifled—show of joy is not immediately
obvious to the daughter who believes herself to
be one stranger approaching another.

All this is by way of saying that Ingrid had
apparently not seen this brief reaction of Eva's, or
if she had seen it, had not been much moved by
it. Ingrid walked with a young man of about her
own age (whom Eva imagined, correctly, to be a
classmate), and soon drew near the house.

Eva struggled to remain calm—to be, as she felt she must be, a stranger. She knew that she would hear her daughter's young voice soon, but when the words came it was still a strange shock.

"Is it true what they say? That you knew my mother?"

Eva, who was by now sitting in her rocking chair, nodded and bade the young woman to come up onto the porch.

"Ya. It is true."

Ingrid gasped.

"Did you hear? Did you hear, Toby? She knew her!"

"I heard," the boy said warily.

"Come here, come here," Eva said. "Sit by me."

Ingrid hesitated for a moment, then drew closer. Presently she fell to her knees and looked up at the older woman. One of her young hands rested comfortably, and

without apparent thought, on Eva's knee. Ingrid took a deep breath before framing with words the question she had come to pose.

"How did you know my mother?"

But Eva said nothing, only smiled and touched the blonde hair. How shiny it was!

The young woman seemed perplexed not to receive an answer; when Eva made a movement toward her, she started for a moment, and then thought better of her fear.

Eva carefully extended her hand toward the soft young neck and touched a string of beads resting there. Then without breaking the movement for an instant, she put her hand to her own neck and removed an identical string of beads.

"She gave you her beads!" Ingrid exclaimed. "I remember, oh, I remember playing with them the morning we landed in America. Hers exactly like mine! And I took hers and put them on my neck, and wound mine about hers! Oh, I remember it so well!"

"I saw you play vit dem as you say," Eva said quietly.

"Then you were on the same ship?"

Eva nodded.

"Tell me, what did Ingrid look like as a little girl?" It was the young man who posed the question. "Miss Parsley said I should ask you."

Eva thought for a moment and asked, "Did dis Miss Parsley give you also dat little bag you have brought?"

He seemed surprised at the directness of the question. "Why, yes," he said.

"Who knows what's come over her," Ingrid said wearily. "She gave him all kinds of orders on a little slip of paper, and wouldn't show me a thing."

"Den she iss a good voman."

The youngsters looked quizzically at her.

"Ingrid vas the morning she came to America wearing a leetle skirt, blue. The bag. Open it, young lady, I tink you vill find it."

He brought the bag. It was as she said. Eva stretched out her hand and took the small blue skirt that Ingrid held out to her, then held it as one would hold a baby. She looked back at Ingrid.

"What else?" the young man asked.

"A leetle bodice, cut vit an angle, lots of squares. Edges, de edges vit flowers. I saw your mother ven she sew dis."

Ingrid withdrew something from the bag, stood up, and held a flowered garment against her breast.

"Oh, you *were* there, you *did* know my mother!" Ingrid shouted. "And you say you saw her sewing this? Oh, how marvelous! Miss Parsley,

when she taught me to sew, would always tell me, 'Now, Ingrid, we must sew with stitches as small as your mother's, you know.'"

"Do you haff, in dat bag, de leetle shoes?"

"Did you hear that, Toby? Of course we have the little shoes. Hand them to me, Toby."

They were wrapped in a colored neckerchief. Toby handed them to Ingrid, who handed them to Eva.

"They are lovely things, you know. They have a high front, and blue leather in the back, and . . ."

"And haff leetle brass clasps, front and back. And a deep scratch on the right shoe by de heel, one or two inches long."

There was a silence as Ingrid regarded her, then opened up the neckerchief and displayed the shoes, which were exactly as they had been described. Eva turned away, ostensibly to look out at the houses on the street, but, more

evidently than she imagined, eager at this point not to have to look another in the eye.

"Diss is vat your mother told me," Eva said, still staring away.

"Toby, leave us here," Ingrid said, wiping away a tear with the back of her hand. The boy left.

"Who are you?" The young woman's question was not pained, not insistent, nor yet even touched with longing. It was the question of one trying to make sense of the forgotten objects of a room after a long night of dreaming.

"I am Crazy Eva," came the answer. "I am a woman by myself here for people to hate. I tink maybe you haff neffer news of your mother without you come on me like this, by a mistake. By an accident. So iss for dat, at least, good dat we should meet." She still would not look Eva in the eye.

"Tell me about my mother," Ingrid said. "Tell me everything you know."

"Tell *me*," said Eva. "You tell me. Vat it iss you remember." She stared down. The waving grain in the painted planks of the porch on which the two women stood ran in long, irregular patterns, rising and falling. It was as though the wooden veins, no two alike, were racing on a course that no one could predict, a course that comprehended any number of paths, a course concluded in itself at the hard seam of each board, and then began anew.

"I remember a gate, a black iron gate," Ingrid responded, as if hypnotized. "I remember a hard bench and a crowd and an iron gate, all black, that took her away."

"Notting more?"

"Nothing more."

They stared out at the cold sky.

"Dere vas more," Eva said.

"Then tell me." Ingrid spoke the words openly, with no fear, as one following a path.

"Your mother, maybe you have thought to hate her for leaving you. But I know she not mean to leave you dere. I know. She vent to ask from a friend a question. And a man at de gate ask to see her ticket. And he said 'Dot's good, go' and push her. Denn a crowd come following a call from someone. Many bodies. She try to get back. Hard, hard, hard, she try to get back. She called you. Den she pushed on dat train, and den gone and no one to talk to."

"She called your name again and again and again."

"She vould be glad you are still called by dat name."

Ingrid stepped closer to her mother. The two were now side by side, a handswidth at most between them, staring out from the porch toward the great grey sky.

"I never hated my mother," Ingrid said softly.

Eva said nothing.

"I had no ticket. All I had was this. Half of an immigration ticket." And she knelt down and pulled from the little bag an old faded ticket.

"A new country," said Eva.

"Yes, it was," said Ingrid.

Ingrid stood up again, pocketed the ticket, and put her hand on Eva's. The older woman closed her eyes and took a deep breath.

Ingrid touched Eva's cheek. "Please look at me," she said.

They were soft, grey-blue eyes, eyes that remembered, eyes that needed, suddenly, no further summoning.

"These beads," Ingrid said, "belonged to you, I think."

And with that Ingrid removed the beads from around her neck and handed them to Eva, who took them in her hand and turned them for a moment. They were round beads, suitable for praying, for reaching beyond oneself, for touching the quiet part of the soul that we see, now and again, in ourselves and in others at Christmas time. The beads were black and round and worn, and the hand that held them seemed to draw the bright essence of life from their scratched dark surfaces.

When the two embraced, it was not difficult at all. It was extended across a gulf of time and distance and words, as true embraces often are, and so they did their best to squeeze every moment of time, every inch of distance, and every syllable of speech out of themselves, to forget such petty details as who they were or had been, and to find again what they had found in the beginning, to

find it over and over and for the first time, as well.
The mother and daughter in each other's arms
tried to stay true to the unspoken demands of a
single heart, a heart that discovers itself again
quite by accident, and in a moment. They tried to
touch something that could only change you if you
tried, like a fool, to put a word on
it, to use language as though it
were not, in the end, a dark
black gate into which true
experience often passed myste-
riously and for an eon. And for
a long moment they did touch something, and it
did not change.

   Word of what happened spread like wildfire
through the town. On Christmas Day, the children
rushed to the Parsley house and cheered and

pointed at Eva (no one called her by her old
name any more), who was waving to them from

an upper window.

Words, of course, had their
place, and there were many that
passed once Eva had made her
way within that house. She
learned, for instance, of the many efforts Miss
Parsley had made to locate her, of the years of
placing advertisements at Christmas time in
Boston's papers and those of nearly every other
city in the country. And Miss Parsley learned of
the hardships and trials Eva had undergone, of
her wanderings and her penury, and of her final,
seemingly aimless decision to settle in the humble
town in upstate New York where they now found
themselves. The tellings and explainings spun
themselves out like tops. At last there was a flat
current of silence, and it was natural. They were
free to simply stare at the exquisitely decorated

tree Miss Parsley had prepared, free not to bother any more with words. Perhaps it was the season before them that explained their comfort with this state of affairs, or perhaps it was the day's remarkable events. For whatever reason, the three women seemed, at long last, to have entered a world in which neither miracles nor accidents—or the words to describe them—were possible or necessary, but only the day at hand.

There was a knock at the door. Miss Parsley rang James's bell and, when he arrived, pointed down the flight of stairs. He nodded and walked down.

When James opened the door, he saw a small boy bearing a huge basket of fruit.

"It's for Miss Ingrid, sir, if you please," the boy chanted, as though he had rehearsed his speech a dozen times or more. "We were hoping we could come to see her this

morning, myself and some of her other friends."
(Here it may be mentioned that Ingrid had, and
had always had, an uncommon facility with the
local children, and was close to nearly every
one of them who lived in the town.) James
thanked the boy, asked him to wait where he
was, and went upstairs to take the basket of fruit
to Miss Parsley.

"I heard him, James, thank you," Miss Parsley
said. She was busy writing something, and did not
look up. "You may place the basket beneath
the tree. Go and return to our young
gift-bearer the gracious thanks of
this house, and tell him to bring
his friends back in half an hour.
Miss Ingrid will have something to
say for us all then, I believe. After
you've seen him off, I want you to prepare a room
for Eva. She will be living with us here now."

James nodded and exited.

"I believe it is beginning to snow," said Ingrid, who was standing by the window next to her mother.

"Clean snow, snow for de day iss good. Vash clean everyting and hold it, hold it vit big vite arms." Eva grasped her daughter's hands.

"Indeed it is," said Miss Parsley, looking up for a moment. She saw the two others staring at each other and smiling. She smiled herself, and then resumed her work.

Perhaps 10 minutes passed in silence.

When Miss Parsley had finished writing, she walked to the window, and the three watched the grey sky shatter open into denser and denser fields of white snowflakes, a gateway limitlessly exposed.

Some time later the doorbell rang. Ingrid opened it and wished the children a merry Christmas, and was wished the same in return by a chorus of young voices.

"I have something important to read to you all," she said.

The children laughed and shouted. Their many voices rang out into the cold white air. "A story!" "How wonderful!" "Ingrid is going to read us a story!" "What kind of story, Ingrid?"

"I must warn you, it's a story without an ending," she answered. And she began to read what Miss Parsley had written.

"'There were two sets of travelers. The first traveler was a grimy old man, ill-shaven, ill-clad, and he often stank of whisky and old cigar smoke. He rode boxcars and begged or stole for his supper. Most people feared him and would not look him in his eye, and thought nothing of it, but the more they looked away the more he became the man they feared.

"'The second set of travelers was made up of a poor man and his wife, who was great with

child. The two had not a penny to their name, and the wife's time was approaching on a bitterly cold night. They had nowhere to go at the time of their greatest need, and no one to see to them. They went from inn to inn, but all the inns were full, and each innkeeper looked away from them and shut the door in their face. To be cast aside by the world at such a time! How do you imagine they felt?

"'I am afraid this is not a once-upon-a-time story. It is a once-upon-many-times story. For the first traveler travels tonight, as do any number of others, and the man and his wife traveled many centuries ago. But their journey, children, was upon the same earth we all share.

"'And our job is not to finish either story, but to begin each one, and all such stories, as that woman's child would have us begin them. With a look in the eye, unjudging and unjudged, and a hand extended in common humanity. To do so is

not an ending, but a beginning, and this day we celebrate the great beginning, the great gift of our own ability to make beginnings together, in the face of adversity and happiness alike.'"

When she had finished she put away the paper, wished the children a merry Christmas, hugged them all, and sent them on their way. And she knew, as she watched them go, that new beginnings do indeed lie somewhere in all of us.

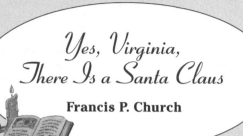

Yes, Virginia, There Is a Santa Claus

Francis P. Church

Editor Francis P. Church's letter to Virginia O'Hanlon is one of the most touching written demonstrations of the importance in believing in what cannot be seen, touched, or proven. The letter originally appeared in the September 21, 1897 edition of the New York Sun. *More than a century later, it remains a classic.*

E TAKE PLEASURE in answering at once and thus prominently the communication below, expressing at the same time our great gratification that its faithful author is numbered among the friends of the *Sun*.

DEAR EDITOR—

I am 8 years old. Some of my little friends say there is no SANTA CLAUS. Papa says, 'If you see it in the Sun it's so.' Please tell me the truth, is there a SANTA CLAUS?

VIRGINIA O'HANLON,
115 West Ninety-Fifth Street.

Virginia, your friends are wrong. They have been affected by the skepticism of a skeptical age. They do not believe except they see. They think that nothing can be which is not comprehensible by their little minds. All minds, Virginia, whether they be men's or children's, are little. In this great universe of ours man is a mere insect, an ant, in his intellect, as compared with the boundless world about him, as measured by the intelligence capable of grasping the whole of truth and knowledge.

Yes, Virginia, there is a Santa Claus. He exists as certainly as love and generosity and devotion exist, and you know that they abound and give to your life its highest beauty and joy. Alas! how dreary would be the world if there were no Santa Claus! It would be as dreary as if there were no Virginias. There would be no childlike faith then,

no poetry, no romance to make tolerable this existence. We should have no enjoyment, except in sense and sight. The eternal light with which childhood fills the world would be extinguished.

Not believe in Santa Claus! You might as well not believe in fairies! You might get your papa to hire men to watch in all the chimneys on Christmas Eve to catch Santa Claus, but even if they did not see Santa Claus coming down, what would that prove? Nobody sees Santa Claus, but that is no sign that there is no Santa Claus. The most real things in the world are those that neither children nor men can see. Did you ever see fairies dancing on the lawn? Of course not, but that's no proof that they are not there.

Nobody can conceive or imagine all the wonders there are unseen and unseeable in the world.

You tear apart the baby's rattle and see what makes the noise inside, but there is a veil covering the unseen world which not the strongest man, nor even the united strength of all the strongest men that ever lived, could tear apart. Only faith, fancy, poetry, love, romance, can push aside that curtain and view and picture the supernal beauty and glory beyond. Is it all real? Ah, Virginia, in all this world there is nothing else real and abiding.

No Santa Claus? Thank God he lives, and he lives forever. A thousand years from now, Virginia, nay, ten times ten thousand years from now, he will continue to make glad the heart of childhood.

The Adventure of the Blue Carbuncle

Sir Arthur Conan Doyle

How does Sherlock Holmes celebrate the holiday season? By getting to the bottom of a mysterious misdeed, of course! Here is one of the classic Holmes stories—with a Christmas setting, no less. The goose that figures prominently in this tale was a staple of the late nineteenth-century Christmas celebration in many households.

 HAD CALLED UPON my friend Sherlock Holmes upon the second morning after Christmas, with the intention of wishing him the compliments of the season. He was lounging upon the sofa in a purple dressing gown, a pipe-rack within his reach upon the right, and a pile of crumpled morning papers, evidently newly studied, near at hand. Beside the couch was a wooden chair, and on the angle on the back hung a very seedy and disreputable felt hat, much the worse for the wear, and cracked in several places. A lens and forceps lying upon the seat of the chair suggested that the hat had been suspended in this manner for the purpose of examination.

"You are engaged," said I; "Perhaps I interrupt you."

"Not at all. I am glad to have a friend with whom I can discuss my results. The matter is a perfectly trivial one"—he jerked his thumb in the direction of the old hat—"but there are points in

connection with it which are not entirely devoid
of interest and even instruction."

I seated myself in his armchair and warmed
my hands before his crackling fire, for a sharp
frost had set in, and the windows were thick with
the ice crystals. "I suppose," I remarked, "that,
homely as it looks, this thing has some deadly
story linked on to it—that it is the clue which will
guide you in the solution of some mystery and
the punishment of some crime."

"No, no. No crime," said Sherlock Holmes,
laughing. "Only one of those whimsical little
incidents which will happen when you have four
million human beings all jostling each other
within the space of a few
square miles. Amid the action
and reaction of so dense a
swarm of humanity, every possible combination of events
may be expected to take

place, and many a little problem will be presented which may be striking and bizarre without being criminal. We have already had experience of such."

"So much so," I remarked, "that of the last six cases which I have added to my notes, three have been entirely free of any legal crime."

"Precisely. You allude to my attempt to recover the Irene Adler papers, to the singular case of Miss Mary Sutherland, and to the adventure of the man with the twisted lip. Well, I have no doubt that this small matter will fall into the same innocent category. You know Peterson, the commissionaire?"

"Yes."

"It is to him that this trophy belongs."

"It is his hat?"

"No, no; he found it. Its owner is unknown. I beg that you will look upon it not as a battered billycock but as an intellectual problem. And, first,

as to how it came here. It arrived upon Christmas morning, in company with a good fat goose, which is, I have no doubt, roasting at this moment in front of Peterson's fire. The facts are these: about four o'clock on Christmas morning, Peterson, who as you know, is a very honest fellow, was returning from some small jollification and was making his way homeward down Tottenham Court Road. In front of him he saw, in the gaslight, a tallish man, walking with a slight stagger, and carrying a white goose hung over his shoulder. As he reached the corner of Goodge Street, a row broke out between this stranger and a little knot of roughs. One of the latter knocked off the man's hat, on which he raised his stick to defend himself and, swinging it over his head, smashed the shop window behind him. Peterson had rushed forward to protect the stranger from his assailants; but the man, shocked at having broke the window, and seeing an official-looking person in uniform rushing towards him,

dropped his goose, took to his heels, and vanished amid the labyrinth of small streets which lie at the back of Tottenham Court Road. The roughs had also fled at the appearance of Peterson, so that he was left in the possession of the field of battle, and also of the spoils of victory in the shape of this battered hat and a most unimpeachable Christmas goose."

"Which surely he restored to their owner?"

"My dear fellow, there lies the problem. It is true that 'For Mrs. Henry Baker' was printed upon a small card which was tied to the bird's left leg, and it is true that the initials 'H.B.' are legible upon the lining of this hat; but as there are some thousands of Bakers, and some hundreds of Henry Bakers in this city of ours, it is not easy to restore lost property to any one of them."

"What, then, did Peterson do?"

"He brought round both hat and goose to me on Christmas morning, knowing that even the

smallest problems are of interest to me. The goose we retained until this morning, when there were signs that, in spite of the slight frost, it would be well that it should be eaten without unnecessary delay. Its finder has carried off, there-fore, to fulfill the ultimate destiny of a goose, while I continue to retain the hat of the unknown gentleman who lost his Christmas dinner."

"Did he not advertise?"

"No."

"Then, what clue could you have as to his identity?"

"Only as much as we can deduce."

"From his hat?"

"Precisely."

"But you are joking. What can you gather from this old battered felt?"

"Here is my lens. You know my methods. What can you gather yourself as to the individu-ality of the man who has worn this article?"

I took the tattered object in my hands and turned it over rather ruefully. It was a very ordinary black hat of the usual round shape, hard and much the worse for wear. The lining had been of red silk, but was a good deal discolored. There was a maker's name; but, as Holmes had remarked, the initials "H.B." were scrawled upon one side. It was pierced in the brim for a hat-securer, but the elastic was missing. For the rest, it was cracked, exceedingly dusty, and spotted in several places, although there seemed to have been some attempt to hide the discolored patches by smearing them with ink.

"I can see nothing," said I, handing it back to my friend.

"On the contrary, Watson, you can see everything. You fail, however, to reason from what you see. You are too timid in drawing your inferences."

"Then pray tell me what it is that you can infer from this hat?"

He picked it up and gazed at it in the peculiar introspective fashion which was characteristic of him. "It is perhaps less suggestive than it might have been," he remarked, "and yet there are a few inferences which are very distinct, and a few others which represent at least a strong balance of probability. That the man was highly intellectual is of course obvious upon the face of it, and also that he was fairly well-to-do within the last three years, although he has now fallen upon evil days. He had foresight, but has less now than formerly, pointing to a moral resignation, which, when taken with the decline of his fortunes, seems to indicate some evil influence, probably drink, at work upon him. This may account also for the obvious fact that his wife has ceased to love him."

"My dear Holmes!"

"He has, however, retained some degree of self-respect," he continued, disregarding my remonstrance. "He is a man who leads a sedentary life, goes out little, is out of training entirely, is middle-aged, has grizzled hair which he has had cut within the last few days, and which he anoints with lime cream. These are the more patent facts which are to be deduced from his hat. Also, by the way, that it is extremely improbably that he has gas laid on in his house."

"You are certainly joking, Holmes."

"Not in the least. Is it possible that even now, when I give you these results, you are unable to see how they are attained?"

"I have no doubt that I am very stupid, but I must confess that I am unable to follow you. For example, how did you deduce that this man was intellectual?"

For answer Holmes clapped the hat upon his head. It came right over the forehead and settled

upon the bridge of his nose. "It is a question of
cubic capacity," said he; "a man with so large a
brain must have something in it."

"The decline of his fortunes, then?"

"This hat is three years old. These flat brims
curled at the edges came in then. It is a hat of
the very best quality. Look at the band of ribbed
silk and the excellent lining. If this man could
afford to buy so expensive a hat three years ago,
and has had no hat since, then he has assuredly
gone down in the world."

"Well, that is clear enough, certainly. But how
about the foresight and the moral regression?"

Sherlock Holmes laughed. "Here is the foresight," he said, putting his finger upon the little
disc and loop of the hat-securer. "They are never
sold upon hats. If this man ordered one, it is a
sign of a certain amount of foresight, since he
went out of his way to take the precaution against
the wind. But since we see that he has broken

the elastic and has not troubled to replace it, it is obvious that he has less foresight now than formerly, which is a distinct proof of a weakening nature. On the other hand, he has endeavored to conceal some of these stains upon the felt by daubing them with ink, which is a sign that he has not entirely lost his self-respect."

"Your reasoning is certainly plausible."

"The further points, that he is middle-aged, that his hair is grizzled, that it has been recently cut, and that he uses lime cream, are all to be gathered from a close examination of the lower part of the lining. The lens discloses a large number of hair-ends, clean cut by the scissors of the barber. They all appear to be adhesive, and there is a distinct odour of lime-cream. This dust, you will observe, is not the gritty, gray dust of the street but the fluffy brown dust of the house, showing that it has been hung up indoors most of the time; while the marks of moisture upon the

inside are proof positive that the wearer perspired freely, and could, therefore, hardly be in the best of training."

"But his wife—You said that she had ceased to love him."

"This hat has not been brushed for weeks. When I see you, my dear Watson, with a week's accumulation of dust upon your hat, and when your wife allows you to go out in such a state, I shall fear that you have also been unfortunate enough to lose your wife's affection."

"But he might be a bachelor."

"Nay, he was bringing home the goose as a peace-offering to his wife. Remember the card upon the bird's leg."

"You have an answer for everything. But how on earth do you deduce that the gas is not laid on in his house?"

"One tallow stain, or even two, might come by chance; but when I see no less than five, I

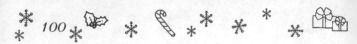

think that there can be little doubt that the individual must be brought into frequent contact with burning tallow-walks upstairs at night probably with his hat in one hand and a guttering candle in the other. Anyhow, he never got tallow-stains from a gas-jet. Are you satisfied?"

"Well, it is very ingenious," said I, laughing; "but since, as you said just now, there has been no crime committed, and no harm done save the loss of a goose, all this seems to be rather a waste of energy."

Sherlock Holmes had opened his mouth to reply, when the door flew open, and Peterson, the commissionaire, rushed into the apartment with flushed cheeks and the face of a man who is dazed with astonishment.

"The goose, Mr. Holmes! The goose, sir!" he gasped.

"Eh? What of it, then? Has it returned to life and flapped off through the kitchen window?"

Holmes twisted himself round upon the sofa to get a fairer view of the man's excited face.

"See here, sir! See what my wife found in its crop!" He held out his hand and displayed upon the center of the palm a brilliantly scintillating blue stone, rather smaller than a bean in size, but of such purity and radiance that it twinkled like an electric point in the dark hollow of his hand.

Sherlock Holmes sat up with a whistle. "By Jove, Peterson!" said he, "This is a treasure trove indeed. I suppose you know what you have got?"

"A diamond, sir? A precious stone. It cuts into glass as though it were putty."

"It's more than a precious stone. It is *the* precious stone."

"Not the Countess of Morcar's blue carbuncle!" I ejaculated.

"Precisely so. I ought to know its size and shape, seeing that I have read the

advertisement about it in the *Times* every day lately. It is absolutely unique, and its value can only be conjectured, but the reward offered of a thousand pounds is certainly not within a twentieth part of the market price."

"A thousand pounds! Great Lord of mercy!" The commissionaire plumped down into the chair and stared from one to the other of us.

"That is the reward, and I have reason to know that there are sentimental considerations in the background which would induce the Countess to part with half her fortune if she could but recover the gem."

"It was lost, if I remember aright, at the Hotel Cosmopolitan," I remarked.

"Precisely so, on December 22nd, just five days ago. John Horner, a plumber, was accused of having abstracted it from the lady's jewel case. The evidence against him was so strong that the case has been referred to the Assizes. I have

some account of this matter here, I believe." He rummaged amid his newspaper, glancing over the dates, until at last he smoothed one out, doubled it over, and read the following paragraph:

Hotel Cosmopolitan Jewel Robbery. John Horner, 26, plumber, was brought up on the charge of having upon the 22nd inst., abstracted from the jewel-case of the Countess of Morcar the valuable gem known as the blue carbuncle. James Ryder, upper-attendant at the hotel, gave his evidence to the effect that he had shown Horner up to the dressing-room of the Countess of Morcar upon the day of the robbery in order that he might solder the second bar of the grate, which was loose. He had remained with Horner some little time, but had finally been called away. On returning, he

found that Horner had disappeared, that the bureau had been forced open, and that the small morocco casket in which, as it afterwards transpired, the Countess was accustomed to keep her jewel, was lying empty on the dressing-table. Ryder instantly gave the alarm, and Horner was arrested the same evening; but the stone could not be found either upon his person or in his rooms. Catherine Cusack, maid to the Countess, deposed to having heard Ryder's cry of dismay on discovering the robbery, and to have rushed into the room, where she found matters as described by the last witness. Inspector Bradstreet, B division, gave evidence as to the arrest of Horner, who struggled frantically, and protested his innocence in the strongest terms. Evidence of a previous conviction for

robbery having been given against the prisoner, the magistrate refused to deal summarily with the offence, but referred it to the Assizes. Horner, who had shown signs of intense emotion during the proceedings, fainted away at the conclusion and was carried out of the court.

"Hum! So much for the police-court," said Holmes thoughtfully, tossing aside the paper. "The question for us now to solve is the sequence of events leading from a rifled jewel-case at one end to the crop of a goose at Tottenham Court Road at the other. You see, Watson, our little deductions have suddenly assumed a much more important and less innocent aspect. Here is the stone; the stone came from the goose, and the goose came from Mr. Henry Baker, the gentleman with the bad hat and all the other characteristics with which I have bored you. So now we must set ourselves

very seriously to finding this gentleman and ascertaining what part he has played in this little mystery. To do this, we must try the simplest means first, and these lie undoubtedly in an advertisement in all the evening papers. If this fails, I shall have recourse to other methods."

"What will you say?"

"Give me a pencil and that slip of paper. Now then:

Found at the corner of Goodge Street, a goose and a black felt hat. Mr. Henry Baker can have the same by applying at 6:30 this evening at 221B Baker Street.

"That is clear and concise."

"Very. But will he see it?"

"Well, he is sure to keep an eye on the papers, since, to a poor man, the loss was a heavy one. He was clearly so scared by his

mischance in breaking the window and by the approach of Peterson that he thought nothing but flight, but since then he must have bitterly regretted the impulse which caused him to drop his bird. Then, again, the introduction of his name will direct his attention to it. Here you are, Peterson, run down to the advertising agency and have this put in the evening papers."

"In which, sir?"

"Oh, in the *Globe*, *Star*, *Pall Mall*, *St. James*, *Evening News Standard*, *Echo*, and any others that occur to you."

"Very well, sir. And this stone?"

"Ah, yes, I shall keep the stone. Thank you. And, I say, Peterson, just buy a goose on your way back and leave it here with me, for we must have one to give to this gentleman in place of the one which your family is now devouring."

When the commissionaire had gone, Holmes took up the stone and held it against the light.

"It's a bonny thing," he said. "Just see how it glints and sparkles. Of course it is a nucleus and focus of crime. Every good stone is. They are the devil's pet baits. In the larger and older jewels every facet may stand for a bloody deed. This stone is not yet twenty years old. It was found in the banks of the Amoy River in southern China and is remarkable in having every characteristic of the carbuncle, save that it is blue in shade instead of ruby red. In spite of its youth, it has already a sinister history. There have been two murders, a vitriol-throwing, a suicide, and several robberies brought about for the sake of this forty-grain weight of crystallized charcoal. Who would think that so pretty a toy would be a purveyor to the gallows and the prison? I'll lock it up in my strong box now and drop a line to the Countess to say that we have it."

"Do you think that this man Horner is innocent?"

"I cannot tell."

"Well, then, do you imagine that this other one, Henry Baker, had anything to do with the matter?"

"It is, I think, much more likely that Henry Baker is an absolutely innocent man, who had no idea that the bird which he was carrying was of considerably more value than if it were made of solid gold. That, however, I shall determine by a very simple test if we have an answer to our advertisement."

"And you can do nothing until then?"

"Nothing."

"In that case, I shall continue my professional round. But I shall come back in the evening at the hour you have mentioned, for I should like to see the solution of so tangled a mess."

"Very glad to see you. I dine at seven. There is a woodcock, I believe. By the way, in view of the recent occurrences, perhaps I ought to ask Mrs. Hudson to examine its crop."

I had been delayed at a case, and it was a little after half-past six when I found myself in Baker Street once more. As I approached the house I saw a tall man in a Scotch bonnet with coat which was buttoned up to his chin waiting outside in the bright semicircle which was thrown from the fanlight. Just as I arrived the door opened, and we were shown up together to Holmes's room. "Mr. Henry Baker, I believe," said he, rising from his armchair and greeting his visitor with the easy air of geniality which he could so readily assume. "Pray take this chair by the fire, Mr. Baker. It is a cold night, and I observe that your circulation is more adapted for summer than for winter. Ah, Watson, you have just come at the right time. Is that your hat, Mr. Baker?"

"Yes sir, that is undoubtedly my hat."

He was a large man with rounded shoulders, a massive head, and a broad, intelligent face, sloping down to a pointed beard of grizzled brown. A touch of red in the nose and cheeks, with a slight

tremor of his extended hand, recalled Holmes's sur-
mise as to his habits. His rusty black frock-coat was
buttoned right up in front, with the collar turned up,
and his lank wrists protruded from his sleeves
without a sign of cuff or shirt. He spoke in a slow
staccato fashion, choosing words with care, and gave
the impression generally of a man of learning and letters who had ill-usage at the hands of fortune.

"We have retained these things for some days,"
said Holmes, "because we expected to see an advertisement from you giving your address. I am at a
loss to know now why you did not advertise."

Our visitor gave a rather shamefaced laugh.
"Shillings have not been so plentiful with me as they
once were," he remarked. "I had no doubt that the
gang of roughs who assaulted me
had carried off both my hat and
the bird. I did not care to spend
more money in a hopeless
attempt at recovering them."

"Very naturally. By the way, about the bird, we were compelled to eat it."

"To eat it!" Our visitor half rose from his chair in his excitement.

"Yes, it would have been of no use to anyone had we not done so. But I presume that this other goose upon the sideboard, which is about the same weight and perfectly fresh, will answer your purpose equally well?"

"Oh, certainly, certainly," answered Mr. Baker with a sigh of relief.

"Of course, we still have the feathers, legs, crop, and so on of your own bird, so if you wish—"

The man burst into a hearty laugh. "They might be useful to me as relics of my adventure," said he, "but beyond that I can hardly see what use the *disjecta membra* of my late acquaintance are going to be to me. No, sir, I think that, with your permission, I will confine my attentions to the excellent bird which I perceive upon the sideboard."

Sherlock Holmes glanced sharply across at me with a slight shrug of the shoulders.

"There is your hat, then, and there is your bird," said he. "By the way, would it bore you to tell me where you got the other one from? I am somewhat of a fowl fancier, and I have seldom seen a better grown goose."

"Certainly sir," said Baker, who had risen and tucked his newly gained property under his arm. "There are a few of us who frequent the Alpha Inn, near the Museum—we are to be found in the Museum itself during the day, you understand. This year our good host, Windigate by name, instituted a goose club, by which, on consideration of some few pence every week, we were each to receive a bird at Christmas. My pence were duly paid, and the rest is familiar to you. I am much indebted to you, sir, for a Scotch bonnet is fitted neither to my years not my gravity." With a comical pomposity of manner he

bowed solemnly to both of us and strode off upon his way.

"So much for Mr. Henry Baker," said Holmes when he had closed the door behind him. "It is quite certain that he knows nothing whatsoever about the matter. Are you hungry, Watson?"

"Not particularly."

"Then I suggest that we turn our dinner into a supper and follow up this clue while it is still hot."

"By all means." It was a bitter night, so we drew on our ulsters and wrapped cravats about our throats. Outside, the stars were shining coldly in a cloudless sky, and the breath of the passers-by blew out into smoke like so many pistol shots. Our footfalls rang out crisply and loudly as we swung through the doctor's quarter, Wimpole Street, Harley Street, and so through Wigmore Street into Oxford Street. In a quarter of an hour we were in Bloomsbury at the Alpha Inn, which is a small public-house at the corner of one of the

streets which runs down into Holborn. Holmes pushed open the door of the private bar and ordered two glasses of beer from the ruddy-faced, white-aproned landlord.

"Your beer should be excellent if it is as good as your geese," said he.

"My geese!" The man seemed surprised.

"Yes. I was speaking only half an hour ago to Mr. Henry Baker, who was a member of your goose club."

"Ah! Yes, I see. But you see, sir, them's not *our* geese," said he.

"Indeed! Whose, then?"

"Well, I got the two dozen from a salesman in Covent Garden."

"Indeed? I know some of them. Which was it?"

"Breckinridge is his name."

"Ah! I don't know him. Well, here's your good health, landlord, and prosperity to your house. Goodnight."

"Now for Mr. Breckinridge," he continued, buttoning up his coat as we came out into the frosty air. "Remember, Watson, that though we have so homely a thing as a goose at one end of this chain, we have at the other a man who will certainly get seven years' penal servitude unless we can establish his innocence. It is possible that our inquiry may but confirm his guilt; but in any case, we have a line of investigation which has been missed by the police, and which a singular chance has placed in our hands. Let us follow it out to the bitter end. Faces to the south, then, and quick march!"

We passed across Holborn, down Endell Street, and so through a zigzag of slums to Covent Garden Market. One of the largest stalls bore the name of Breckinridge upon it, and the proprietor, a horsy-looking man, with a sharp face and trim side whiskers, was helping a boy to put up the shutters.

"Good-evening. It's a cold night," said Holmes.

The salesman nodded and shot a questioning look at my companion.

"Sold out of geese, I see," continued Holmes, pointing at the bare slabs of marble.

"Let you have five hundred to-morrow morning."

"That's no good."

"Well, there are some on the stall with the gas-flare."

"Ah, but I was recommended to you."

"Who by?"

"The landlord of the Alpha."

"Oh, yes; I sent him a couple of dozen."

"Fine birds they were, too. Now where did you get them from?"

To my surprise the question provoked a burst of anger from the salesman.

"Now, then, mister," said he, with his head cocked and his arms akimbo, "what are you driving at? Let's have it straight now."

"It is straight enough. I should like to know who sold you the geese which you supplied to the Alpha."

"Well, then, I shan't tell you. So now!"

"Oh, it is a matter of no importance; but I don't know why you should be so warm over such a trifle."

"Warm! You'd be as warm, maybe, if you were as pestered as I am. When I pay good money for a good article there should be an end of the business; but it's 'Where are the geese?' and 'Who did you sell the geese to?' and 'What will you take for the geese?' One would think they were the only geese in the world, to hear the fuss that is made over them."

"Well, I have no connection with any other people who have been making inquiries," said Holmes carelessly. "If you won't tell us the bet is off, that is all. But I'm always ready to back my opinion on a matter of fowls, and I have a fiver on it that the bird I ate is a country bred."

"Well, then, you've lost your fiver, for it's town bred," snapped the salesman. "It's nothing of the kind."

"I say it is."

"I don't believe it."

"D'you think you know more about fowls than I, who have handled them ever since I was a nipper? I tell you, all those birds that went to the Alpha were town bred."

"You'll never persuade me to believe that."

"Will you bet, then?"

"It's merely taking your money, for I know that I am right. But I'll have a sovereign on with you, just to teach you not to be so obstinate."

The salesman chuckled grimly. "Bring me the books, Bill," said he.

The small boy brought round a small thin volume and a great greasy-backed one, laying them out together beneath the hanging lamp.

"Now, then, Mr. Cocksure," said the salesman, "I thought that I was out of geese, but before I finish you'll find that there is still one left in my shop. You see this little book?"

"Well?"

"That's the list of the folk from whom I buy. D'you see? Well, then, here on this page are the country folk, and the numbers after their names are where their accounts are in the big ledger. Now, then! You see this other page in red ink? Well, that is a list of my town suppliers. Now, look at that third name. Just read it out to me."

"Mrs. Oakshott, 117, Brixton Road—249," read Holmes.

"Quite so. Now turn that up in the ledger."

Holmes turned to the page indicated. "Here you are, 'Mrs. Oakshott, 117, Brixton Road, egg and poultry supplier.'"

"Now, then, what's the last entry?"

"'December 22nd. Twenty-four geese at 7s.6.'"

"Quite so. There you are. And underneath?"

"'Sold to Mr. Windigate of the Alpha, at 12s.'"

"What have you to say now?"

Sherlock Holmes looked deeply chagrined. He drew a sovereign from his pocket and threw it down upon the slab, turning away with the air of a man whose disgust is too deep for words. A few yards off he stopped under a lamp-post and laughed in the hearty, noiseless fashion which was peculiar to him.

"When you see a man with whiskers of that cut and in 'Pink 'un' protruding out of his pocket, you can always draw him out of a bet," said he. "I dare say that if I had put a hundred pounds in front of him, that man would not have given me such complete information as was drawn from him by the idea that he was doing me on a wager. Well, Watson, we are, I fancy, nearing the

end of our quest, and the only point which remains to be determined is whether we should go on to this Mrs. Oakshott tonight, or whether we should reserve it for to-morrow. It is clear from what that surly fellow said that there are others besides ourselves who are anxious about the matter, and I should—"

His remarks were suddenly cut short by a loud hubbub which broke out from the stall which we had just left. Turning round we saw a little rat-faced fellow standing in the center of the circle of yellow light which was thrown by the swinging lamp, while Breckinridge, the salesman, framed in the door of his stall, was shaking his fists fiercely at the cringing figure.

"I've had enough of you and your geese," he shouted. "I wish you were all at the devil together. If you come pestering me any more with your silly talk I'll set the dog at you. You bring Mrs. Oakshott here and I'll answer her, but what have

you to do with it? Did I buy the geese off you?"

"No, but one of them was mine all the same," whined the little man.

"Well, then, ask Mrs. Oakshott for it."

"She told me to ask you."

"Well, you can ask the King of Proosia, for all I care. I've had enough of it. Get out of this!" He rushed fiercely forward, and the inquirer flitted away into the darkness.

"Ha! This man may save us a visit to Brixton Road," whispered Holmes. "Come with me, and we will see what is to be made of this fellow." Striding through the scattered knots of people who lounged round the flaring stalls, my companion speedily overtook the little man and touched him on the shoulder. He sprang round, and I could see in the gas-light that every vestige of color had been driven from his face.

"Who are you, then? What do you want?" he asked in a quavering voice.

"You will excuse me," said Holmes blandly, "but I could not help overhearing the questions which you put to the salesman just now. I think that I could be of assistance to you."

"You? Who are you? How could you know anything of this matter?"

"My name is Sherlock Holmes. It is my business to know what other people don't know."

"But you can know nothing of this?"

"Excuse me, I know everything of it. You are endeavoring to trace some of the geese which were sold by Mrs. Oakshott, of Brixton Road, to a salesman named Breckinridge, by him in turn to Mr. Windigate of the Alpha, and by him to his club, of which Mr. Henry Baker is a member."

"Oh, sir, you are the very man whom I have longed to meet," cried the little fellow with outstretched hands and quivering fingers. "I can hardly explain to you how interested I am in this matter."

Sherlock Holmes hailed a four-wheeler which was passing. "In that case we had better discuss it in a cosy room rather than in this wind-swept market-place," said he. "But pray tell me, before we go far-ther, who it is that I have the pleasure of assisting."

The man hesitated for an instant. "My name is John Robinson," he answered with a sidelong glance.

"No, no, the real name," said Holmes sweetly. "It is always awkward doing business with an alias."

A flush sprang to the white cheeks of the stranger. "Well, then," said he, "my real name is James Ryder."

"Precisely so. Head attendant at the Hotel Cosmopolitan. Pray step into the cab, and I shall soon be able to tell you everything which you wish to know."

The little man stood glancing from one to the other of us with half-frightened, half-hopeful eyes, as one who is not sure whether he is on the verge of a windfall or a catastrophe. Then he stepped into

the cab, and in half an hour we were back in the
sitting-room at Baker Street. Nothing had been
said during our drive, but the high, thin breathing
of our new companion, and the claspings and
unclaspings of his hands, spoke of the nervous
tension within him.

"Here we are!" said Holmes cheerily as we
filed into the room. "The fire looks very seasonable
in this weather. You look cold, Mr. Ryder. Pray take
the basket-chair. I will just put on my slippers before
we settle this little matter of yours. Now, then! You
want to know what became of those geese?"

"Yes, sir."

"Or rather, I fancy, of that goose. It was one
bird, I imagine, in which you were interested—
white, with a black bar across the tail."

Ryder quivered with emotion. "Oh, sir," he
cried, "can you tell me where it went to?"

"It came here."

"Here?"

"Yes, and a most remarkable bird it proved. I don't wonder that you should take an interest in it. It laid an egg after it was dead—the bonniest, brightest little blue egg that ever was seen. I have it here in my museum."

Our visitor staggered to his feet and clutched the mantelpiece with his right hand. Holmes unlocked the strong-box and held up the blue carbuncle, which shone out like a star, with a cold, brilliant, many-pointed radiance. Ryder stood glaring with a drawn face, uncertain whether to claim or disown it.

"The game's up, Ryder," said Holmes quietly. "Hold up, man, or you'll be into the fire! Give him an arm back into his chair, Watson. he's not got blood enough to go in for felony with impunity. Give him a dash of brandy. So! Now he looks a little more human. What a shrimp it is, to be sure!"

For a moment he had staggered and nearly
fallen, but the brandy brought a tinge of colour
into his cheeks, and he sat staring with frightened
eyes at his accuser.

"I have almost every link in my hands, and
all the proofs which I could possibly need, so
there is little which you need to tell me. Still, that
little may as well be cleared up to make the case
complete. You had heard, Ryder, of this blue
stone of the Countess of Morcar's?"

"It was Catherine Cusack who told me of it,"
said he in a crackling voice.

"I see—her ladyship's waiting-maid. Well, the
temptation of sudden wealth so easily acquired
was too much for you, as it has been for better
men before you; but you were not very scrupulous
in the means you used. It seems to me, Ryder,
that there is the making of a very pretty villain in
you. You knew that this man Horner, the plumber,
had been concerned in some such matter before,

and that suspicion would rest the more readily upon him. What did you do, then? You made some small job in my lady's room—you and your confederate Cusack—and you managed that he should be the man sent for. Then, when he had left, you rifled the jewel-case, raised the alarm, and had this unfortunate man arrested. You then—"

Ryder threw himself down suddenly upon the rug and clutched at my companion's knees. "For God's sake, have mercy!" he shrieked. "Think of my father! of my mother! It would break their hearts. I never went wrong before! I never will again. I swear it. I'll swear it on a Bible. Oh, don't bring it into court! For Christ's sake, don't!"

"Get back into your chair!" said Holmes sternly. "It is very well to cringe and crawl now, but you thought little enough of this poor Horner in the dock from a crime of which he knew nothing."

"I will fly, Mr. Holmes. I will leave the country, sir. Then the charges against him will break down."

"Hum! We will talk about that. And now let us hear a true account of the next act. How came the stone into the goose, and how came the goose into the open market? Tell us the truth, for there lies your only hope of safety."

Ryder passed his tongue over his parched lips. "I will tell you just as it happened, sir," he said. "When Horner had been arrested, it seemed to me that it would be best for me to get away with the stone at once, for I did not know at what moment the police might take it into their heads to search me and my room. There was no place about the hotel where it would be safe. I went out, as if on some commission, and I made for my sister's house. She had married a man named Oakshott, and lived on Brixton Road, where she fattened fowls for the market. All the way there every man I met seemed to me to be a policeman or a detective; and, for all that it was a cold night, the sweat was pouring down my face before I came to the

Brixton Road. My sister asked me what was the matter, and why I was so pale; but I told her that I had been upset by the jewel robbery at the hotel. Then I went into the backyard and smoked a pipe, and wondered what it would be best to do.

"I had a friend once called Maudsley, who went to the bad, and has just been serving his time in Pentonville. One day he had met me, and fell into talk about the ways of thieves, and how they could get rid of what they stole. I knew that he would be true to me, for I knew one or two things about him; so I made up my mind to go right on to Kilburn, where he lived, and take him into my confidence. He would show me how to turn the stone into money. But how to get to him in safety? I thought of the agonies I had gone through in coming from the hotel. I might at any moment be seized and searched, and there would be the stone in my waistcoat pocket. I was leaning against the wall at the time and looking at the geese which

were waddling round my feet, and suddenly an idea came into my head which showed me how I could beat the best detective that ever lived.

"My sister had told me some weeks before that I might have the pick of her geese for a Christmas present, and I knew that she was always as good as her word. I would take my goose now, and in it I would carry the stone to Kilburn. There was a little shed in the yard, and behind this I drove one of the birds—a fine big one, white, with a barred tail. I caught it, and, prying its bill open, I thrust the stone down its throat as far as my finger could reach. The bird gave a gulp, and I felt the stone pass along its gullet and down into its crop. But the creature flapped and struggled, and out came my sister to know what was the matter. As I turned to speak to her, the brute broke loose and fluttered among the others.

"'Whatever were you doing with that bird, Jem?' says she.

"'Well,' said I, 'you said you'd give me one for Christmas, and I was feeling which was the fattest.'

"'Oh,' says she, 'we've set yours aside for you—Jem's bird, we call it. It's the big white one over yonder. There's twenty-six of them, which makes one for you, and one for us, and two dozen for the market.'

"'Thank you, Maggie,' says I; 'but if it is all the same to you, I'd rather have that one I was handling just now.'

"'The other one is a good three pound heavier,' said she, 'and we fattened it expressly for you.'

"'Never mind. I'll have the other, and I'll take it now,' said I.

"'Oh, just as you like,' said she, a little huffed. 'Which is it you want, then?'

"'That white one with the barred tail, right in the middle of the flock.'

"'Oh, very well. Kill it and take it with you.'

"Well, I did what she said, Mr. Holmes, and I carried the bird all the way to Kilburn. I told my pal what I had done, for he was a man that it was easy to tell a thing like that to. He laughed until he choked, and we got a knife and opened the goose. My heart turned to water, for there was no sign of the stone, and I knew some terrible mistake had occurred. I left the bird, rushed back to my sister's, and hurried into the back yard. There was not a bird to be seen there.

"'Where are they all, Maggie?' I cried.

"'Gone to the dealer's, Jem.'

"'Which dealer's?'

"'Breckinridge, of Covent Garden.'

"'But was there another with a barred tail? I asked, 'the same as the one I chose?'

"'Yes, Jem; there were two barred-tailed ones, and I could never tell them apart.'

"Well, then, of course I saw it all, and I ran off as hard as my feet would carry me to this

man Breckinridge; but he had sold the lot at once, and not one word would he tell me as to where they had gone. You heard him yourselves to-night. Well, he has always answered me like that. My sister thinks that I am going mad. Sometimes I think that I am myself. And now— and now I am myself a branded thief, without ever having touched the wealth for which I sold my character. God help me! God help me!" He burst into convulsive sobbing, with his face buried in his hands.

There was a long silence, broken only by his heavy breathing, and by the measured tapping of Sherlock Holmes' finger-tips upon the edge of the table. Then my friend rose and threw open the door.

"Get out!" said he.

"What, sir! Oh, Heaven bless you!"

"No more words. Get out!"

And no more words were needed. There was a rush, a clatter upon the stairs, the bang of a door, and the crisp rattle of running footfalls from the street.

"After all, Watson," said Holmes, reaching up his hands for his clay pipe, "I am not retained by the police to supply their deficiencies. If Horner were in danger it would be another thing; but this fellow will not appear against him, and the case must collapse. I suppose that I am committing a felony, but it is just possible that I am saving a soul. This fellow will not go wrong again; he is too terribly frightened. Send him to jail now, and you make him a jail-bird for life. Besides, it is the season for forgiveness. Chance has put in our way a most singular and whimsical problem, and its solution is its own reward."

The Elves and the Shoemaker

The Brothers Grimm

Though Jacob and Wilhelm Grimm devoted their lives to the study of literature, they never wrote any of the stories that won them world renown. The tales that made them famous, Der Kinder und Hausmärchen (The Children and the House of Fairy Tales) *were collected from the European folklore and legends of the time. While "The Elves and the Shoemaker" stands on its own as a fairy tale, it is also an example of how an act of selfless giving has the power to change lives for the better.*

NCE UPON A TIME there was a poor
shoemaker. He made excellent shoes
and worked quite diligently, but even so
he could not earn enough to support himself and
his family. He became so poor that he could not
even afford to buy the leather he needed to make
shoes; finally he had only enough to make one
last pair. He cut them out with great care and put
the pieces on his workbench, so that he could
sew them together the following morning.

"Now, I wonder," he sighed, "will I ever make
another pair of shoes? Once I've sold this pair I
shall need all the money to buy food for my
family. I will not be able to buy any new leather."

That night, the shoemaker went to bed a sad
and distraught man.

The next morning, he awoke early and went
down to his workshop. On his bench he found
an exquisite pair of shoes! They had small and
even stitches, formed so perfectly that he knew

he couldn't have produced a better pair himself. Upon close examination, the shoes proved to be made from the very pieces of leather he had set out the night before. He immediately put the fine pair of shoes in the window of his shop and drew back the blinds.

"Who in the world could have done this service for me?" he asked himself. Even before he could make up an answer, a rich man strode into his shop and bought the shoes—and for a fancy price.

The shoemaker was ecstatic; he immediately went out and purchased plenty of food for his family—and some more leather. That afternoon he cut out two pairs of shoes and, just as before, laid all the pieces on his bench so that he could sew them the next day.

Then he went upstairs to enjoy a good meal with his family.

"My goodness!" he cried the next morning when he found two pairs of beautifully finished shoes on his workbench. "Who could make such fine shoes—and so quickly?" He put them in his shop window, and before long some wealthy people came in and paid a great deal of money for them. The happy shoemaker went right out and bought even more leather.

For weeks, and then months, this continued. Whether the shoemaker cut two pairs or four pairs, the fine new shoes were always ready the next morning. Soon his small shop was crowded with customers. He cut out many types of shoes: stiff boots lined with fur, delicate slippers for dancers, walking shoes for ladies, tiny shoes for children. Soon his shoes had bows and laces and

buckles of fine silver The little shop prospered as never before, and its proprietor was soon a rich man himself. His family wanted for nothing.

As the shoemaker and his wife sat by the fire one night, he said, "One of these days, I shall learn who has been helping us."

"We could hide behind the cupboard in your workroom," she said. "That way, we would find out just who your helpers are." And that is just what they did. That evening, when the clock struck twelve, the shoemaker and his wife heard a noise. Two tiny men, each with a bag of tools, were squeezing beneath a crack under the door. Oddest of all, the two elves were stark naked!

The two men clambered onto the workbench and began working. Their little hands stitched and their little hammers tapped ceaselessly the whole night through.

"They are so small! And they make such beautiful shoes in no time at all!" the shoemaker whispered to his wife as dawn rose. (Indeed, the elves were about the size of his own needles.)

"Quiet!" his wife answered. "See how they are cleaning up now." And in an instant, the two elves had disappeared beneath the door.

The next day, the shoemaker's wife said, "Those little elves have done so much good for us. Since it is nearly Christmas, we should make some gifts for them."

"Yes!" cried the shoemaker. "I'll make some boots that will fit them, and you make some clothes." They worked until dawn. On Christmas Eve the presents were laid out upon the work-bench: two tiny jackets, two pairs of trousers, and two little woolen caps. They also left out a plate of good things to eat and drink. Then they hid

once again behind the cupboard and waited to
see what would happen.

Just as before, the elves appeared at the
stroke of midnight. They jumped onto the bench
to begin their work, but when they saw all the
presents they began to laugh and shout with joy.
They tried on all the clothes, then helped themselves to the food and drink. Then they jumped
down, danced excitedly around the workroom,
and disappeared beneath the door.

After Christmas, the shoemaker cut out his
leather as he always had—but the two elves never
returned. "I believe they may have heard us whis-
pering," his wife said. "Elves are so very shy
when it comes to people,
you know."

"I know I will miss
their help," the shoemaker
said, "but we will manage.
The shop is always so

busy now. But my stitches will never be as tight and small as theirs!"

That shoemaker did indeed continue to prosper, but he and his family always remembered the good elves who had helped them during the hard times. And each and every Christmas Eve from that year onward, they gathered around the fire to drink a toast to their tiny friends.

The Gift of the Magi

O. Henry

*"The Gift of the Magi" is probably the best
known of all O. Henry's works, and it's
not hard to see why. The story, which features a classic example of the ironic end-
ings that made the author famous, captures
the essence of the spirit of Christmas. The
poor young couple in the story, like their
Biblical counterparts, leave an unforgettable
impression, thanks to the pureness of their
intent, the selflessness of their giving, and
the power of their love.*

NE DOLLAR AND 87 cents. That was all. And 60 cents of it was in pennies. Pennies saved one and two at a time by bulldozing the grocer and vegetable man and the butcher until one's cheeks burned with the silent imputation of parsimony that such close dealing implied. Three times Della counted it. One dollar and 87 cents. And the next day would be Christmas.

There was clearly nothing to do but flop down on the shabby little couch and howl. So Della did it. Which instigates the moral reflection that life is made up of sobs, sniffles, and smiles, with sniffles predominating.

While the mistress of the home is gradually subsiding from the first stage to the second, take a look at the home. A furnished flat at eight dollars per week. It did not exactly beggar description, but it certainly had that word on the lookout for the mendicancy squad.

In the vestibule below was a letter-box into which no letter would go, and an electric button from which no mortal finger could coax a ring. Also appertaining thereunto was a card bearing the name "Mr. James Dillingham Young."

The "Dillingham" had been flung to the breeze during a former period of prosperity when its possessor was being paid 30 dollars per week. Now, when the income was shrunk to 20 dollars, the letters of "Dillingham" looked blurred, as though they were thinking seriously of contracting to a modest and unassuming D. But whenever Mr. James Dillingham Young came home and reached his flat above he was called "Jim" and greatly hugged by Mrs. James Dillingham Young, already introduced to you as Della. Which is all very good.

Della finished her cry and attended to her cheeks with a powder puff. She stood by the window and

looked out dully at a gray cat walking a gray fence in a gray back yard. Tomorrow would be Christmas Day, and she had only $1.87 to buy Jim a present. She had been saving every penny she could for months, with this result. Twenty dollars a week doesn't go far. Expenses had been greater than she had calculated. They always are. Only $1.87 to buy a present for Jim. Her Jim. Many a happy hour she had spent planning for something nice for him. Something fine and rare and sterling—something just a little bit near to being worthy of the honor of being owned by Jim.

There was a pier glass between the windows of the room. Perhaps you have seen a pier glass in an eight-dollar flat. A very thin and very agile person may, by observing his reflection in a rapid sequence of longitudinal strips, obtain a fairly accurate conception of his looks. Della, being slender, had mastered the art.

Suddenly she whirled from the window and stood before the glass. Her eyes were shining brilliantly, but her face had lost its color within 20 seconds. Rapidly she pulled down her hair and let it fall to its full length.

Now, there were two possessions of the James Dillingham Youngs in which they both took a mighty pride. One was Jim's gold watch that had been his father's and his grandfather's. The other was Della's hair. Had the Queen of Sheba lived in the flat across the airshaft, Della would have let her hair hang out the window some day to dry just to depreciate Her Majesty's jewels and gifts. Had King Solomon been the janitor, with all his treasures piled up in the basement, Jim would have pulled out his watch every time he passed, just to see him pluck at his beard from envy.

So now Della's beautiful hair fell about her, rippling and shining like a cascade of brown waters. She did it up again nervously and quickly. Once she faltered for a minute while a tear splashed on the worn red carpet.

On went her old brown jacket; on went her old brown hat. With a whirl of skirts and with the brilliant sparkle still in her eyes, she fluttered out the door and down the stairs to the street.

Where she stopped the sign read: "Mme. Sofronie. Hair Goods of All Kinds." One flight up Della ran, and collected herself, panting. Madame, large, too white, chilly, hardly looked the "Sofronie."

"Will you buy my hair?" asked Della.

"I buy hair," said Madame. "Take yer hat off and let's have a sight at the looks of it." Down rippled the brown cascade. "Twenty dollars," said Madame, lifting the mass with a practiced hand.

"Give it to me quick," said Della. Oh, and the

next two hours tripped on rosy wings. Forget
the hashed metaphor. She was ransacking the
stores for Jim's present.

She found it at last. It surely had been
made for Jim and no one else. There was no
other like it in any of the stores, and she had
turned all of them inside out. It was a platinum
watch-chain, simple and chaste in design, properly proclaiming its value by substance alone
and not by meretricious ornamentation—as all
good things should do. It was even worthy of
The Watch. As soon as she saw it she knew
that it must be Jim's. It was like him. Quietness
and value—the description applied to both.
Twenty-one dollars they took from her for it,
and she hurried home with the 87 cents. With
that chain on his watch Jim might be properly
anxious about the time in any company. Grand
as the watch was, he sometimes looked at it
on the sly on account of the shabby old

leather strap that he used in place of a proper gold chain.

When Della reached home her intoxication gave way a little to prudence and reason. She got out her curling-irons and lighted the gas and went to work repairing the ravages made by generosity added to love. Which is always a tremendous task, dear friends—a mammoth ask.

Within 40 minutes her head was covered with tiny close-lying curls that made her look wonderfully like a truant schoolboy. She looked at her reflection in the mirror long, carefully, and critically.

"If Jim doesn't kill me," she said to herself, "before he takes a second look at me, he'll say I look like a Coney Island chorus girl. But what could I do—oh! what could I do with a dollar and 87 cents?"

At seven o'clock the coffee was made and the frying pan was on the back of the stove, hot and ready to cook the chops. Jim was never late, Della doubled the watch chain in her hand and sat on the corner of the table near the door that he always entered. Then she heard his step on the stair away down on the first flight, and she turned white for just a moment. She had a habit of saying little silent prayers about the simplest everyday things, and now she whispered: "Please, God, make him think I am still pretty."

The door opened and Jim stepped in and closed it. He looked thin and very serious. Poor fellow, he was only 22—and to be burdened with a family! He needed a new overcoat and he was without gloves.

Jim stepped inside the door, as immovable as a setter at the scent of quail. His eyes

were fixed upon Della, and there was an expression in them that she could not read, and it terrified her. It was not anger, nor surprise, nor disapproval, nor horror, nor any of the sentiments that she had been prepared for. He simply stared at her fixedly with that peculiar expression on his face.

Della wriggled off the table and went for him. "Jim, darling," she cried, "don't look at me that way. I had my hair cut off and sold it because I couldn't have lived through Christmas without giving you a present. It'll grow out again—you won't mind, will you? I just had to do it. My hair grows awfully fast. Say 'Merry Christmas!' Jim, and let's be happy. You don't know what a nice—what a beautiful gift I've got for you."

"You've cut off your hair?" asked Jim, laboriously, as if he had not arrived at that patent fact yet even after the hardest mental labor.

"Cut it off and sold it," said Della. "Don't you like me just as well, anyhow? I'm me without my hair, ain't I?" Jim looked about the room curiously. "You say your hair is gone?" he said, with an air almost of idiocy. "You needn't look for it," said Della. "It's sold, I tell you—sold and gone, too. It's Christmas Eve, boy. Be good to me, for it went for you. Maybe the hairs of my head were numbered," she went on with a sudden serious sweetness, "but nobody could ever count my love for you. Shall I put the chops on, Jim?"

Out of his trance Jim seemed to quickly wake. He enfolded his Della. For 10 seconds let us regard with discreet scrutiny some inconsequential object in the other direction. Eight dollars a week or a million a year—what is the difference? A mathematician or a wit would give you the

wrong answer. The Magi brought valuable gifts, but that was not among them. This dark assertion will be illuminated later on.

Jim drew a package from his overcoat pocket and threw it upon the table. "Don't make any mistake, Dell," he said, "about me. I don't think there's anything in the way of a haircut or a shave or a shampoo that could make me like my girl any less. But if you'll unwrap that package you may see why you had me going awhile at first."

White fingers and nimble tore at the string and paper. And then an ecstatic scream of joy; and then, alas! a quick feminine change to hysterical tears and wails, necessitating the immediate employment of all the comforting powers of the lord of the flat.

For there lay The Combs—the set of combs that Della had worshiped for long in a Broadway window. Beautiful combs, pure tortoise shell, with

jeweled rims—just the shade to wear in the beautiful vanished hair. They were expensive combs, she knew, and her heart had simply craved and yearned over them without the least hope of possession. And now they were hers, but the tresses that should have adorned the coveted adornments were gone.

But she hugged them to her bosom, and at length she was able to look up with dim eyes and a smile and say: "My hair grows so fast, Jim!"

And then Della leaped up like a little singed cat and cried, "Oh, oh!" Jim had not yet seen his beautiful present. She held it out to him eagerly upon her open palm. The dull precious metal seemed to flash with a reflection of her bright and ardent spirit.

"Isn't it a dandy, Jim? I hunted all over town to find it. You'll have to look at the time a hundred times a day now.

Give me your watch. I want to see how it looks on it."

Instead of obeying, Jim tumbled down on the couch and put his hands under the back of his head and smiled. "Dell," said he, "let's put our Christmas presents away and keep 'em awhile. They're too nice to use just at present. I sold the watch to get the money to buy your combs. And now suppose you put the chops on."

The Magi, as you know, were wise men—wonderfully wise men—who brought gifts to the Babe in the manger. They invented the art of giving Christmas presents. Being wise, their gifts were no doubt wise ones, possibly bearing the privilege of exchange in case of duplication. And here I have

lamely related to you the uneventful chronicle of two foolish children in a flat who most unwisely sacrificed for each other the greatest treasures of their house. But in a last word to the wise of these days let it be said that of all who give gifts these two were the wisest. Of all who give and received gifts, such as they are wisest. Everywhere they are the wisest. They are the Magi.

The Legend of the Christmas Rose

Selma Lagerlof

*Although there are a number of versions
of this tale, Selma Lagerlof's is one of the
most popular. With its emphasis on the
exiled thieves, her story demonstrates that
the spirit of Christmas can bring even the
darkest souls to light.*

ROBBER MOTHER, who lived in Robbers' Cave up in Goinge forest, went down to the village one day on a begging tour. Robber Father, who was an outlawed man, did not dare to leave the forest. She took with her five youngsters, and each youngster bore a sack on his back as long as himself. When Robber Mother stepped inside the door of a cabin, no one dared refuse to give her whatever she demanded; for she was not above coming back the following night and setting fire to the house if she had not been well received. Robber Mother and her brood were worse than a pack of wolves, and many a man felt like running a spear through them; but it was never done, because they all knew that the man stayed

up in the forest, and he would have known how to wreak vengeance if anything had happened to the children or the old woman.

Now that Robber Mother went from house to house and begged, she came to Ovid, which at that time was a cloister. She rang the bell of the cloister gate and asked for food. The watchman let down a small wicket in the gate and handed her six round bread cakes—one for herself and one for each of the five children.

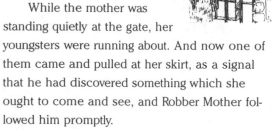

While the mother was standing quietly at the gate, her youngsters were running about. And now one of them came and pulled at her skirt, as a signal that he had discovered something which she ought to come and see, and Robber Mother followed him promptly.

The entire cloister was surrounded by a high and strong wall, but the youngster had managed to find a little back gate that stood ajar. When Robber Mother got there, she pushed the gate

open and walked inside without asking leave, as it was her custom to do.

Ovid Cloister was managed at that time by Abbot Hans, who knew all about herbs. Just within the cloister wall he had planted a little herb garden, and it was into this that the old woman had forced her way.

At first glance Robber Mother was so astonished that she paused at the gate. It was high summertide, and Abbot Hans' garden was so full of flowers that the eyes were fairly dazzled by the blues, reds, and yellows, as one looked into it. But presently an indulgent smile spread over her features, and she started to walk up a narrow path that lay between many flowerbeds.

In the garden a lay brother walked about, pulling up weeds. It was he who had left the door in the wall open,

that he might throw the weeds and tares on the rubbish heap outside.

When he saw Robber Mother coming in, with all five youngsters in tow, he ran toward her at once and ordered them away. But the beggar woman walked right on as before. The lay brother knew of no other remedy than to run into the cloister and call for help.

He returned with two stalwart monks, and Robber Mother saw that now it meant business! She let out a perfect volley of shrieks, and, throwing herself upon the monks, clawed and bit at them; so did all the youngsters. The men soon learned that she could overpower them, and all they could do was to go back into the cloister for reinforcements.

As they ran through the passageway that led to the cloister, they met Abbot Hans, who came rushing out to learn what all this noise was about.

He upbraided them for using force and forbade their calling for help. He sent both monks back to

their work, and although he was an old and fragile man, he took with him only the lay brother.

He came up to the woman and asked in a mild tone if the garden pleased her.

Robber Mother turned defiantly toward Abbot Hans, for she expected only to be trapped and overpowered. But when she noticed his white hair and bent form, she answered peaceably, "First, when I saw this, I thought I had never seen a prettier garden; but now I see that it can't be compared with one I know of. If you could see the garden of which I am thinking you would uproot all the flowers planted here and cast them away like weeds."

The Abbot's assistant was hardly less proud of the flowers than the Abbot himself, and after hearing her remarks he laughed derisively.

Robber Mother grew crimson with rage to think that her word was doubted, and she cried out: "You monks, who are holy men, certainly

must know that on every Christmas Eve the great Goinge forest is transformed into a beautiful garden, to commemorate the hour of our Lord's birth. We who live in the forest have seen this happen every year. And in that garden I have seen flowers so lovely that I dared not lift my hand to pluck them."

Ever since his childhood, Abbot Hans had heard it said that on every Christmas Eve the forest was dressed in holiday glory. He had often longed to see it, but he had never had the good fortune. Eagerly he begged and implored Robber Mother that he might come up to the Robbers' Cave on Christmas Eve. If she would only send one of her children to show him the way, he could ride up there alone, and he would never betray them—on the contrary, he would reward them insofar as it lay in his power.

Robber Mother said no at first, for she was thinking of Robber Father and of the peril that might befall him should she permit Abbot Hans to ride up to their cave. At the same time the desire to prove to the monk that the garden that she knew was more beautiful than his got the better of her, and she gave in.

"But more than one follower you cannot take with you," said she, "and you are not to waylay us or trap us, as sure as you are a holy man."

This Abbot Hans promised, and then Robber Mother went her way.

It happened that Archbishop Absalon from Lund came to Ovid and remained through the night. The lay brother heard Abbot Hans telling the Bishop about Robber Father and asking him for a letter of ransom for the man, that he might lead an honest life among respectable folk.

But the Archbishop replied that he did not care to let the robber loose among honest folk in the villages. It would be best for all that he remain in the forest.

Then Abbot Hans grew zealous and told the Bishop all about Goinge forest, which, every year at Yuletide, clothed itself in summer bloom around the Robbers' Cave. "If these bandits are not so bad but that God's glories can be made manifest to them, surely we cannot be too wicked to experience the same blessing."

The Archbishop knew how to answer Abbot Hans. "This much I will promise you, Abbot Hans," he said, smiling, "that any day you send me a blossom from the garden in Goinge forest, I will give you letters of ransom for all the outlaws you may choose to plead for."

The following Christmas Eve Abbot Hans was on his way to the forest. One of the Robber

Mother's wild youngsters ran ahead of him, and close behind him was the lay brother.

It turned out to be a long and hazardous ride. They climbed steep and slippery side paths, crawled over swamp and marsh, and pushed through windfall and bramble. Just as daylight was waning, the robber boy guided them across a forest meadow, skirted by tall, naked leaf trees and green fir trees. Back of the meadow loomed a mountain wall, and in this wall they saw a door of thick boards. Now Abbot Hans understood that they had arrived, and dismounted. The child opened the heavy door for him, and he looked into a poor mountain grotto, with bare stone walls. Robber

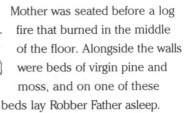

Mother was seated before a log fire that burned in the middle of the floor. Alongside the walls were beds of virgin pine and moss, and on one of these beds lay Robber Father asleep.

"Come in, you out there!" shouted Robber Mother without rising, "and fetch the horses in with you, so they won't be destroyed by the night cold."

Abbot Hans walked boldly into the cave, and the lay brother followed. Here were wretchedness and poverty and nothing was done to celebrate Christmas.

Robber Mother spoke in a tone as haughty and dictatorial as any well-to-do peasant woman. "Sit down by the fire and warm yourself, Abbot Hans," said she, "and if you have food with you, eat, for the food which we in the forest prepare you wouldn't care to taste. And if you are tired after the long journey, you can lie down on one of these beds to sleep. You needn't be afraid of oversleeping, for I'm sitting here by the fire keeping watch. I shall awaken you in time to see that which you have come up here to see."

Abbot Hans obeyed Robber Mother and brought forth his food sack; but he was so fatigued after the journey he was hardly able to eat, and as soon as he could stretch himself on the bed, he fell asleep.

The lay brother was also assigned a bed to rest in, and he dropped into a doze. When he woke up, he saw that Abbot Hans had left his bed and was sitting by the fire talking with Robber Mother. The outlawed robber sat also by the fire. He was a tall, raw-boned man with a dull, sluggish appearance. His back was turned to Abbot Hans, as though he would have it appear that he was not listening to the conversation.

Abbot Hans was telling Robber Mother all about the Christmas preparations he had seen on the journey, reminding her of Christmas feasts and games that she must have known in her youth, when she lived at peace with mankind.

At first Robber Mother answered in short, gruff sentences, but by degrees she became more subdued and listened more intently. Suddenly Robber Father turned toward Abbot Hans and shook his clenched fist in his face. "You miserable monk! Did you come here to coax from me my wife and children? Don't you know that I am an outlaw and may not leave the forest?"

Abbot Hans looked him fearlessly in the eyes. "It is my purpose to get a letter of ransom for you from Archbishop Absalon," said he. He had hardly finished speaking when the robber and his wife burst out laughing. They knew well enough the kind of mercy a forest robber could expect from Bishop Absalon!

"Oh, if I get a letter of ransom from Absalon," said Robber Father, "then I'll promise you that never again will I steal so much as a goose."

Suddenly Robber Mother rose. "You sit here and talk, Abbot Hans," she said, "so that we are forgetting to look at the forest. Now I can hear, even in this cave, how the Christmas bells are ringing."

The words were barely uttered when they all sprang up and rushed out. But in the forest it was still dark night and bleak winter. The only thing they marked was a distant clang borne on a light south wind.

When the bells had been ringing a few moments, a sudden illumination penetrated the forest; the next moment it was dark again, and then light came back. It pushed its way forward between the stark trees, like a shimmering mist. The darkness merged into a faint daybreak. Then Abbot Hans saw that the snow had vanished from the ground, as if someone had removed a carpet, and the earth began to take

on a green covering. The moss-tufts thickened and raised themselves, and the spring blossoms shot upward their swelling buds, which already had a touch of color.

Again it grew hazy; but almost immediately there came a new wave of light. Then the leaves of the trees burst into bloom, crossbeaks hopped from branch to branch, and the woodpeckers hammered on the limbs until the splinters fairly flew around them. A flock of starlings from up country lighted in a fir top to rest.

When the next warm wind came along, the blueberries ripened and the baby squirrels began playing on the branches of the trees.

The next light wave that came rushing in brought with it the scent of newly ploughed acres. Pine and spruce trees were so thickly clothed with red cones that they shone like crimson mantles and forest flowers covered the ground till it was all red, blue, and yellow.

Abbot Hans bent down to the earth and broke off a wild strawberry blossom, and, as he straightened up, the berry ripened in his hand.

The mother fox came out of her lair with a big litter of black-legged young. She went up to Robber Mother and scratched at her skirt, and Robber Mother bent down to her and praised her young.

Robber Mother's youngsters let out perfect shrieks of delight. They stuffed themselves with wild strawberries that hung on the bushes. One of them played with a litter of young hares; another ran a race with some young crows, which had hopped from their nest before they were really ready.

Robber Father was standing out on a marsh eating raspberries. When he glanced up, a big black bear stood beside him. Robber Father broke off a twig and struck the bear on the nose. "Keep to your own ground, you!" he said. "This is my turf." The huge bear turned around and lumbered off in another direction.

Then all the flowers whose seeds had been brought from foreign lands began to blossom. The loveliest roses climbed up the mountain wall in a race with the blackberry vines, and from the forest meadow sprang flowers as large as human faces.

Abbot Hans thought of the flower he was to pluck for Bishop Absalon; but each new flower that appeared was more beautiful than the others, and he wanted to choose the most beautiful of all.

Then Abbot Hans marked how all grew still; the birds hushed their songs, the flowers ceased growing, and the young foxes played no more. From far in the distance faint harp tones were heard, and celestial song, like a soft murmur, reached him.

He clasped his hands and dropped to his knees. His face was radiant with bliss.

But beside Abbot Hans stood the lay brother who had accompanied him. In his mind there were dark thoughts. "This cannot be a true miracle," he thought, "since it is revealed to malefactors. This does not come from God, but is sent hither by Satan. It is the Evil One's power that is tempting us and compelling us to see that which has no real existence."

The angel throng was so near now that Abbot Hans saw their bright forms through the forest branches. The lay brother saw them, too; but back of all this wondrous beauty he saw only some dread evil.

All the while the birds had been circling around the head of Abbot Hans, and they let him take them in his hands. But all the animals were afraid of the lay brother; no bird perched on his shoulder, no snake played at his feet. Then there came a little forest dove. When she marked that the angels were nearing, she plucked up courage

and flew down on the lay brother's shoulder and laid her head against his cheek.

Then it appeared to him as if sorcery were come right upon him, to tempt and corrupt him. He struck with his hand at the forest dove and cried in such a loud voice that it rang throughout the forest, "Go thou back to hell, whence thou art come!"

Just then the angels were so near that Abbot Hans felt the feathery touch of their great wings, and he bowed down to earth in reverent greeting.

But when the lay brother's words sounded, their song was hushed and the holy guests turned in flight. At the same time the light and the mild warmth vanished in unspeakable terror for the darkness and cold in a human heart. Darkness sank over the earth, like a coverlet; frost came, all the growths

shrivelled up; the animals and birds hastened away; the leaves dropped from the trees, rustling like rain.

Abbot Hans felt how his heart, which had but lately swelled with bliss, was now contracting with insufferable agony. "I can never outlive this," thought he, "that the angels from heaven had been so close to me and were driven away; that they wanted to sing Christmas carols for me and were driven to flight."

Then he remembered the flower he had promised Bishop Absalon, and at the last moment he fumbled among the leaves and moss to try and find a blossom. But he sensed how the ground under his fingers froze and how the white snow came gliding over the ground. Then his heart caused him even greater anguish. He could not rise, but fell prostrate on the ground and lay there.

When the robber folk and the lay brother had groped their way back to the cave, they

missed Abbot Hans. They took brands with them and went out to search for him. They found him dead upon the coverlet of snow.

When Abbot Hans had been carried down to Ovid, those who took charge of the dead saw that he held his right hand locked tight around some-thing that he must have grasped at the moment of death. When they finally got his hand open, they found that the thing that he had held in such an iron grip was a pair of white root bulbs, which he had torn from among the moss and leaves.

When the lay brother who had accompanied Abbot Hans saw the bulbs, he took them and planted them in Abbot Hans' herb garden.

He guarded them the whole year to see if any flower would spring from them. But in vain he waited through the spring, the summer, and the autumn. Finally, when winter had set in and all

the leaves and the flowers were dead, he ceased caring for them.

But when Christmas Eve came again, he was so strongly reminded of Abbot Hans that he wandered out into the garden to think of him. And look! As he came to the spot where he had planted the bare root bulbs, he saw that from them had sprung flourishing green stalks, which bore beautiful flowers with silver white leaves.

He called out all the monks at Ovid, and when they saw that this plant bloomed on Christmas Eve, when all the other growths were as if dead, they understood that this flower had in truth been plucked by Abbot Hans from the Christmas garden in Goinge forest. Then the lay brother asked the monks if he might take a few blossoms to Bishop Absalon.

When Bishop Absalon beheld the flowers, which had sprung from the earth in darkest winter, he turned as pale as if he had met a

ghost. He sat in silence a moment; thereupon he said, "Abbot Hans has faithfully kept his word and I shall also keep mine."

He handed the letter of ransom to the lay brother, who departed at once for the Robbers' Cave. When he stepped in there on Christmas Day, the robber came toward him with axe uplifted. "I'd like to hack you monks into bits, as many as you are!" said he. "It must be your fault that Goinge forest did not last night dress itself in Christmas bloom."

"The fault is mine alone," said the lay brother, "and I will gladly die for it; but first I must deliver a message from Abbot Hans." And he drew forth the Bishop's letter and told the man that he was free.

Robber Father stood there pale and speechless, but Robber Mother said in his name, "Abbot Hans has indeed kept his word, and Robber Father will keep his."

When the robber and his wife left the cave, the lay brother moved in and lived all alone in the forest, in constant meditation and prayer that his hard-heartedness might be forgiven him.

But Goinge forest never again celebrated the hour of our Saviour's birth; and of all its glory, there lives today only the plant which Abbot Hans had plucked. It has been named Christmas Rose. And each year at Christmastime she sends forth from the earth her green stalks and white blossoms, as if she never could forget that she had once grown in the great Christmas garden at Goinge forest.

A Letter from Santa Claus

Mark Twain

*The father of young Susie Clemens, Samuel
Langhorne Clemens (a.k.a. Mark Twain),
once took pen in hand to craft an unforgettable Christmas offering.*

Palace of St. Nicholas in the Moon
Christmas Morning

MY DEAR SUSIE CLEMENS:

 have received and read all the letters which you and your little sister have written me by the hand of your mother and your nurses; I have also read those which you little people have written me with your own hands—for although you did not use any characters that are in grown people's alphabet, you used the characters that all children in all lands on earth and in the twinkling stars use; and as all my subjects in the moon are children and use no characters but that, you will easily understand that I can read your and your baby sister's jagged and fantastic marks without any trouble at all. But I had trouble with those letters which you dictated through your mother and the

nurses, for I am a foreigner and cannot read
English writing well. You will find that I made no
mistakes about the things which you and the
baby ordered in your own letters—I went down
your chimney at midnight when you were asleep
and delivered them all myself—and kissed both
of you, too, because you are good children, well
trained, nice mannered, and about the most obe-
dient little people I ever saw. But in the letter
which you dictated there were some words
which I could not make out for certain, and one or two small
orders which I could not
fill because we ran out of
stock. Our last lot of
kitchen furniture for dolls
has just gone to a very
poor little child in the North Star away up in the
cold country above the Big Dipper. Your mama
can show you that star and you will say: "Little

Snow Flake" (for that is the child's name), "I'm glad you got that furniture, for you need it more than I." That is, you must write that, with your own hand, and Snow Flake will write you an answer. If you only spoke it she wouldn't hear you. Make your letter light and thin, for the distance is great and the postage very heavy.

There was a word or two in your mama's letter which I couldn't be certain of. I took it to be "a trunk full of doll's clothes." Is that it? I will call at your kitchen door about nine o'clock to inquire. But I must not see anybody and I must not speak to anybody but you. When the kitchen doorbell rings, George must be blind-folded and sent to open the door. Then he must go back to the dining room or the china closet and take the cook with him. You must tell

George he must walk on tiptoe and not speak—
otherwise he will die someday. Then you must
go up to the nursery and stand on a chair or
the nurse's bed and put your ear to the speaking
tube that leads down to the kitchen and when I
whistle through it you must speak in the tube
and say, "Welcome, Santa Claus!" Then I will ask
whether it was a trunk you ordered or not. If
you say it was, I shall ask you what *color* you
want the trunk to be.

Your mama will help you to name a nice
color and then you must tell me every single
thing in detail which you want the trunk to
contain. Then when I say
"Good-by and a merry
Christmas to my little Susie
Clemens," you must say
"Good-by, good old Santa
Claus, I thank you very
much and please tell that

little Snow Flake I will look at her star tonight
and she must look down here—I will be right in
the west bay window; and every fine night I will
look at her star and say, 'I know somebody up
there and *like* her, too.'" Then you must go
down into the library and make George close all
the doors that open into the main hall, and
everybody must keep still for a little while. I will
go to the moon and get those things and in a
few minutes I will come down the chimney that
belongs to the fireplace that is in the hall—if it
is a trunk you want—because I couldn't get such
a thing as a trunk down the nursery chimney,
you know.

People may talk if they want, until they hear
my footsteps in the hall. Then you tell them to
keep quiet a little while till I go back up the
chimney. Maybe you will not hear my footsteps at
all—so you may go now and then and peep
through the dining-room doors, and by and by

you will see that thing which you want, right under the piano in the drawing room—for I shall put it there.

If I should leave any snow in the hall, you must tell George to sweep it into the fireplace, for I haven't time to do such things. George must not use a broom, but a rag—else he will die someday. You must watch George and not let him run into danger. If my boot should leave a stain on the marble, George most not holy-stone it away. Leave it there always in memory of my visit; and whenever you look at it or show it to anybody you must let it remind you to be a good little girl. Whenever you are naughty and somebody points to that mark which your good old Santa Claus's boot made on the marble, what will you say, little sweetheart?

Good-by for a few minutes, till I come down to the world and ring the kitchen doorbell.

Your loving SANTA CLAUS
Whom people sometimes call "The Man in the Moon"